YOU WERE MEANT FOR ME

A SMALL TOWN SOUTHERN ROMANCE

KAIT NOLAN

To my planner-obsessed brethren. This book is for you.

A LETTER TO READERS

Dear Reader,

This book is set in the Deep South. As such, it contains a great deal of colorful, colloquial, and occasionally grammatically incorrect language. This is a deliberate choice on my part as an author to most accurately represent the region where I have lived my entire life. This book also contains swearing and pre-marital sex between the lead couple, as those things are part of the realistic lives of characters of this generation, and of many of my readers.

If any of these things are not your cup of tea, please consider that you may not be the right audience for this book. There are scores of other books out there that are written with you in mind. In fact, I've got a list of some of my favorite authors who write on the sweeter side on my website at https://kaitnolan.com/on-the-sweeter-side/

If you choose to stick with me, I hope you enjoy!

Happy reading!

Kait

CHAPTER 1

"*P*lease fasten your seatbelt, Miss Peyton. We're heading into some turbulence."

Tess's French-manicured fingers clenched the arms of the leather seat as the plane shuddered and bucked. Not because she was afraid of flying—her father's pilot was ex-Air Force and could fly anything—but because the Indian food she'd gotten from that sketchy takeaway on the drive to Heathrow was making a bid to come back up.

You will not throw up. You do not have time for food poisoning.

The evidence of her packed schedule was laid out on the table before her, in all its painstakingly bullet-journaled glory, in the pages of the planner that dictated her life. If it wasn't in the planner, it simply didn't happen. Puking her guts up somewhere over Alabama wasn't in it. Ergo, she would not be sick. End of story. And what Peytons wanted, they usually got if they worked hard enough.

She breathed through the roiling of her stomach and tried to focus on the reports she needed to get through before they landed. Her father would expect an update on the latest London project, and she needed to be on the ball to prove she had not only handled the additional responsibility he'd given her, she'd waded into the shitstorm and made it come up aces. That would be important when she proposed what she really wanted: that he allow her to take a greater role in operations of the home office in Denver.

Not that either of those things was the point of this trip to Mississippi. No, her powerful, successful, brilliant father had moved there to be with his new wife. Tess still couldn't quite wrap her brain around the fact that her dad had gone to *Vegas* of all places. Sure, Peyton Consolidated had a hotel on the strip. But absolutely no one expected multi-billionaire Gerald Peyton, III to be married by an Elvis impersonator wearing *gold lamé*. Video footage had been leaked by a gossip blog and gone viral. Speculation had run rampant. Tess had her own concerns about the haste of the marriage, but during their brief meeting a few months before, when the newlyweds had swung through London on the way home from their Paris honeymoon, she couldn't deny that Sandy seemed to adore her father, and he was likewise smitten. He was *happy*. Happier than she'd ever seen him. It wasn't in her to begrudge him that after the misery of his marriage to her mother.

Hell, she'd envy him if she truly believed a commitment like that was really real and could really last. But she didn't believe it. Not deep down. Six weeks ago she'd had her own shot at that kind of happiness. She'd been looking for adventure. Romance. A chance to step outside the tower walls and be someone besides Tess Peyton, someone without all the attendant responsibilities that went along with the family name. So she'd gone up to Scotland for the weekend, in search of her own hottie Highlander. Except instead of a kilted Scotsman, she'd found an ex-pat American, with a voice like honeyed whiskey and a mouth made for sin. He'd given her everything she'd wanted—and so much more. One night turned into two, then two turned into four, and before she'd known it, a week had gone by. The best damned week of her life.

But her uncharacteristic bid at recklessness, at going off-plan, hadn't ended with wedding bells. It had just ended. She'd seen to that, hadn't she? Nowhere in her planner did it spell out 1) Meet the man of your dreams. 2) Fall in love. Therefore, it hadn't happened. So there was no sense in dwelling on it. No sense remembering the taste of him or the feel of his hand in hers. No sense thinking about how he'd looked, sleeping and sated, the last time she'd seen him. When she found her fingers stroking over the delicate filigree of her necklace—the necklace he'd given her— Tess dropped her hand, shutting down that line of thinking with the same ruthlessness she used to hold back the nausea, and went back to the reports.

By the time she'd white-knuckled her way through half a dozen more pages, the air had smoothed out and so had her stomach.

Jon came over the onboard intercom. "We're about fifteen minutes out, Miss Peyton. Starting our descent."

Thank God. It would still take time to get from the county seat of Lawley out to the tiny town of Wishful, but God willing, she could be face down on the glorious bed in the penthouse at The Babylon in another hour, falling into blessed unconsciousness. Right this moment, nothing sounded better than that.

Flagging where she'd left off, Tess made a few more notes on things to follow up on when she called to check in with her team tomorrow morning. Then she gathered up her paperwork, stowing it neatly in the relevant folders and squaring the edges before sliding the pile into her Italian leather briefcase, alongside her favorite fountain pens. The tidy little MacBook went next, and finally her planner in the outside pocket. By the time the jet touched down, she had her game face on, ready for whatever got thrown at her next.

At least until she stepped off the plane.

Her father was waiting on the tarmac wearing jeans and a long-sleeved polo shirt. On *a work day*. As she descended the short flight of steps, he took off his aviator sunglasses and hooked them into the neck of his shirt, a broad grin lighting his face.

"There's my baby girl!" He scooped her off her feet, all but squeezing the breath out of her.

"Wait a minute!" Her jet-lagged brain was having trouble shifting to seeing the weekend version of her dad during business hours.

He set her down, frowning. "Problem?"

Tess relinquished the briefcase and threw her arms around him, squeezing back. "That's better. Hi, Daddy." She nuzzled her cheek against his shoulder, feeling some of the stress knots relax at the strength of his embrace. She'd cut off a limb before admitting she needed some of his strength right now, but she'd soak it up nonetheless.

"Good flight?"

"Productive. I've got the latest figures on the Piccadilly project and some ideas of how we might cut costs without sacrificing quality."

He waved that off. "All that can wait."

Tess blinked. "Okay then." If he wasn't going to jump immediately into business mode, neither would she.

"Your bag, Miss Peyton. Good afternoon, sir."

She worked up a smile. "Thanks, Jon."

Her father shook the pilot's hand. "Thanks for delivering my daughter safely."

"Always a pleasure."

Tess shouldered the briefcase. "I'll see you next week."

The pilot saluted and headed to do the post-flight check of the jet. Her father grabbed her suitcase and led her toward the terminal.

Tess fell into step beside him. "Is Sandy with you?"

"At home putting together a big family dinner in your honor. Everybody's coming."

"Who exactly is everybody?" She hoped she didn't sound as

wary as she felt, but the idea of peopling after the long flight wasn't remotely appealing.

"The whole family. Sandy's mom, Helen—you're gonna love her. She's a spitfire. Not at all like Grandmother Peyton. Both Sandy's brothers and their wives. Sandy's son and his wife, and all the cousins and their respective significant others." Seeing the wince she couldn't hold back, he laughed. "I know, it's a lot for us, but I promise, you'll get used to it. They're great people, and they can't wait to meet you."

Resigned to the fact that face planting was going to have to wait, Tess looped her arm through her father's. "Then you had better give me the Cliff's Notes bios of everybody so I can keep them all straight."

MITCH CAMPBELL TOOK one look at the coconut cream pie on the diner table and swore. "This is a pie kind of emergency?"

Judd Hamilton laid a protective hand over the clear plastic dome. "Touch this and die. My pregnant wife had a craving, and I am doing my husbandly duty."

Mitch ignored the twinge he felt at the mental image of Judd and Autumn wrapped in connubial bliss. If anybody deserved happiness, it was those two. He slid into the booth on the opposite side. "Then why am I here?"

"Just wait. Liam's on his way."

"Fine." Mitch folded his hands loosely on the table and dug up a smile for the little brunette waitress who sidled up to take his order. The smile took way more effort than it should have. "Hey Hannah, can I get a cup of coffee and a slice of—what else do we have today in the pie department?"

"Apple, chocolate icebox, and Judd here got the last coconut cream."

"Apple is a classic for a reason."

"Warm and a la mode?"

"Is there any other way to eat apple pie?" Dimly, Mitch was aware of the flirtatious grin Hannah shot his way, but he couldn't summon the energy to reply in kind.

"You got it."

As she walked toward the counter, he realized Judd was staring at him. "What?"

"You didn't flirt with her."

"So?" He didn't feel like flirting. That wasn't a crime.

Frowning, Judd shook his head.

"What are we really meeting about? Is this about the design for the nursery? Because I think Liam will kill you if you change it again. You, not Autumn, because we all like your wife."

"He's right," Liam announced, squeezing into the booth beside Mitch. "Your ass I have no problem beating."

"Not the nursery either," Judd said. "It's nearly finished, and she cried buckets over it."

Mitch braced himself. "Good cry or bad cry?"

"Good cry. I think. The preggo hormones make it hard to tell sometimes. Right now, she and Mom are putting their heads together on how to create a girly *Star Wars*-themed room."

"Now *I* might cry. That's beautiful, man." Liam mimed wiping a tear. "You married a helluva woman."

"Yes, yes, I did."

"Looking forward to joining your ranks." Liam relaxed back against the booth, the picture of contentment. "Though I'm starting to think you had the right idea proposing and marrying the girl on the same day. It seems a helluva lot less complicated than planning a wedding."

"I thought your mom and Riley were taking care of all of that," Judd said.

"They are. But I'm expected to have opinions on shit."

Hannah came back with Mitch's pie and coffee and took Liam's order, interrupting the wedding discussion and distracting them from the fact that Mitch had stopped contributing to the conversation.

What could he say? *I wish I could follow you both over that cliff? I want what you have? I thought I had it, but it slipped through my fingers?* None of that was what they expected of him. He was the flirt. The unrepentant lover of women. As all of his friends and cousins had fallen into their forevers, he'd looked on with an increasing sense of bemusement. He'd never be felled so easily.

And yet he had. Hard and fast and irrevocably.

"Afternoon gentlemen." Mama Pearl Buckley, the much-beloved, opinionated heart of Dinner Belles, slid Liam's milkshake onto the table. Her gaze skated over to Mitch's, those dark eyes assessing. After a moment, she nodded to herself, as if confirming something, and Mitch realized she knew. Not the who or the how, but she knew at long last he'd toppled. She'd predicted it right here two years ago, hadn't she?

One of these days, Mitch Campbell, you gonna find yourself one that ruins you for all others, and we all gonna enjoy the show.

Except they didn't get the show because the curtain had already fallen. A week's performance. No reprisals.

Because he'd been the dumbass who'd taken one look at Anna on that tiny pub stage in Edinburgh, singing "Dancing Queen" for all she was worth, and slid right over the edge. When she'd proposed a no strings, no last names affair, he'd agreed without question. She'd dazzled him, plain and simple. Neither of them had planned on more than one night. Neither of them had planned anything. And it had been the freest, most unapologetically himself he'd ever been. By the end of a week, he'd known to the marrow of his bones that he wanted more than just her last name. He wanted everything. But when he woke, intent on convincing her that they were so much more than a simple vacation fling, she'd been gone. His anonymous Anna had disappeared into the ether, as if she'd never been. Except for the indelible mark on his fractured heart.

Judd narrowed his eyes. "Dude, are you humming...ABBA?"

Aw hell, he'd been humming "Dancing Queen" under his breath.

"Is that what that is? I've had an ear worm for days." It was the only lie that might allow him to save face.

Liam angled toward him. "Okay, let's get down to it."

"Yeah, let's." The sooner they finished with whatever this was, the sooner Mitch could get the hell out of here and go...try to find something that would distract him from his misery. Which was becoming increasingly hard to do given he was surrounded by enough new couples to people Noah's freaking ark. Maybe he should think about getting a dog.

"This is an intervention," Judd announced.

"You have not been yourself since you got back from that conference in Paris," Liam added.

Mitch stared at them. "Seriously? This is about me?"

"We're worried about you, man. You're not flirting, not dating, and you skipped poker night." Judd pronounced it like an indictment.

"I had work." They didn't need to know that the plans he was working up were for him and not a client.

"What's going on with you?" Liam asked.

He wasn't telling them about Anna. If he did, it would get back to his large and very nosy family, and there'd be no end to the questions. Not to mention he had no intention of explaining why he'd thought a no strings, no last names affair was a good idea. He could just see his mama shaking her head and tsking, "I raised you better." Yeah, that was not a conversation he wanted to be having. Especially not as gossip moved faster than the speed of light in Wishful, and he was expected at a family dinner in a couple of hours.

But Anna was only part of his funk.

"Excuse me for being less than my usual charming self when I get home from a trip to find out my sister was kidnapped. And that everyone—*everyone*—kept it from me." He still hadn't gotten past that. He'd known somebody was harassing Miranda before he'd left. But she'd insisted it wasn't a big deal, and she was romantically involved with the chief of police. Ethan had given his word nothing would happen to her. So he'd taken the trip. And while Mitch had been abroad, having that life-changing affair, his baby sister had been kidnapped and beaten. Finding out that happened, that he hadn't been home to protect her…it messed with his head.

"The whole thing was over in four hours. There was nothing you could've done," Judd assured him. Not for the first time. As he'd been in on the takedown, he was in a position to know. Not that it made a whit of difference to Mitch.

"And when I called home to say I was extending my trip? Nobody thought I should be read in about the fact that Miranda was in the hospital." He didn't have to manufacture the bitterness in his voice.

"Because the guy who put her there was already dead, and she wanted the chance to heal a bit," Judd continued, as if it was the most reasonable thing in the world. "You know she hates it when you hover. The rest of your family was doing enough of that."

Mitch stabbed up a bite of pie hard enough to send the slice halfway off its plate. "I should have been here."

"What is it you think you could've done that Ethan didn't already do?" Liam asked. "Do you blame him for what happened to her?"

"No." Mitch wasn't arrogant enough to believe that if he'd been home his sister never would have been taken in the first place or that she'd have been found any faster. Ethan had taken a bullet for her. It was hard to think that while they'd both been suffering, he'd been with Anna. Cheerfully oblivious.

"Then what is your deal?" Judd demanded.

If they'd told him, if he'd come home on his normal schedule, he never would have met Anna, and he wouldn't have this damned crater in his heart. Because the Bard was a hundred percent wrong. Loving and losing sucked ass.

"I don't appreciate being cut out." How could she have just *left?*

"Are you seriously going to be a drama queen about this? Because the decision wasn't about you," Judd said.

Not talking about Anna. Pull your head out of your ass.

"I know. Intellectually, I get that. But all of you were here, you went through it, and you processed it. I'm just still working my way through all of that. I'm her brother. I've spent my whole life protecting her. I can't just shake it off." The sense of failure was too great.

Liam nudged him with an elbow. "It wasn't your fault."

"I know that, too. I'll get past it." And he knew he would get past the complicated snarl of emotional shit with his sister, at least. "I'm just...not feeling like any of the things I cared about before matter anymore, and I don't want to just go through the motions."

His friends were silent for a long moment, watching him. Mitch wondered what they saw. Did they really buy that this was all about Miranda?

Judd blew out a breath. "Okay then. Take the time."

"We're here if you need us."

A little of the pressure to perform, to rise to expectations, slid off Mitch's shoulders. He let the corner of his mouth curve. "Are we done with the touchy feely shit now? Because I really just want to finish my pie."

CHAPTER 2

"We're so glad you're here!" Sandy wrapped Tess in a warm hug.

After a long moment, Tess lifted her own arms to awkwardly return the embrace. A part of her wanted to be reserved, out of loyalty to her mother. She didn't know what to do with this open affection from a woman she barely knew. But her mom and her grandmother had instilled manners, no matter what. "Thank you for having me."

As Sandy stepped back, she seemed to flow toward Tess's father and he toward her, until they were linked, arms around each other's waist. A unit. The gesture was so natural, so seemingly in sync. She'd never seen her parents act like that. It was disconcerting and set up some kind of ache inside, as if her inner child was finally having to let go of the idea that they'd ever be a real family again. Which was ridiculous. Her parents had been divorced for more than a decade.

"Almost everybody's here," Sandy said. "My niece, Miranda, and her boyfriend, Ethan, couldn't make it. And my nephew is running late, but everyone else is out back. They're so excited to meet you."

Tess couldn't claim the same level of enthusiasm, but more than a fair chunk of that was the jet lag. She forced a tired smile. "Then let's get to introductions."

The moment they stepped out onto the wide back patio, her mouth dropped open. "Oh my God, there are so many of you."

They laughed and a petite brunette stepped forward, beaming. "It's a little overwhelming at first, but I promise we're all housebroken. I'm Norah Crawford, Sandy's daughter-in-law."

Norah Crawford, formerly Burke, the city planner who'd convinced her father to invest in Wishful in the first place. A woman Tess knew he considered something of a second daughter. Uncertain exactly how she felt about that, Tess extended her hand, taking the other woman's measure. "Pleased to meet you."

Norah shook, her grasp warm as she covered it with her free hand. "I've heard so much about you." She looped her arm through Tess's and began the introductions, starting with a lanky man, whose thick blond hair was about two weeks past needing a cut. "This is my husband, Cam."

"Sandy's son, the city councilman and owner of the nursery," Tess reeled off.

Cam stepped forward and grinned. "And I guess technically your step-brother now."

For a moment, Tess could only stare. Not only because the idea of acquiring a step-brother when she was twenty-six seemed ludicrous, but because something in his smile, in the shape of his hazel eyes was shockingly familiar. For two heartbeats, three, she was back in Scotland seeing a different smile, hearing a different laugh. And that just twisted the knife in the ache that hadn't faded over these past weeks.

Tess blinked and realized she'd been staring a bit too long. Offering a rueful smile, she took Cam's extended hand. "Sorry. It's coming on midnight according to my body clock. I'm a little muzzy headed."

"We'll get this show on the road so you can eat and get some rest," Sandy promised. "Trey, why don't you go ahead and put the steaks on?"

"You got it." Her father disappeared into the kitchen. The *kitchen.* He was going to actually *grill?* And Trey. That was another change she hadn't gotten used to. But Tess realized the nickname suited him more than the formality of Gerald ever had, especially in this more relaxed setting.

Norah's voice pulled her back to the introductions and a studious looking guy in horn rim glasses, who leaned, hip-to-hip, with another brunette. Was everybody in this family paired off? The idea of it made her feel even more alone and isolated than she already had.

"This is Reed—he'd be the youngest Campbell. And this is his fiancée, Cecily Dixon."

Tess shook more hands as she flipped through the mental notes from the descriptions her father had tried to give on the hour-long drive from Lawley—at least the ones before she'd pleaded mental fatigue after the fifth name. In typical Peyton fashion, the only part that had stuck were the business details. "Inglenook Books and Whistlestop Marketing." They nodded. Cecily, Tess remembered, had been Norah's intern in Chicago and followed her down south to relocate, despite her blue-blooded roots in Greenwich.

"This is Jimmy and Anita, Reed's parents. Jimmy is Sandy's middle brother," Norah explained. "And this is Pete, her oldest brother, and his wife Liz."

Tess endured more handshakes and friendly greetings and names that more or less flew right back out of the sieve that was her brain.

"And this is Helen, but everybody calls her Grammy."

The silver-haired sprite, who was the only one present shorter than Norah, stepped forward to wrap Tess in an affectionate squeeze, as if they'd known each other forever and she was just one of the kids. "Welcome, young lady. I'm delighted to have another grandchild to spoil."

Tess faltered. "I...thank you."

How could these people be so open and accepting of a total stranger? Were they really granting her full status in the family just because her dad had married in? The Peyton family certainly didn't operate that way. Tess couldn't imagine Grandmother Peyton doing such a thing without a full check of pedigree.

"It's nice to meet all of you."

"Can I get you something to drink? Water? Wine?" Cam asked.

"Actually, if it wouldn't be too much trouble, coffee. If I don't get some caffeine, I'm not sure I'll make it through dinner."

"On it."

The group broke into some form of controlled chaos, everybody pitching in to do something to ready the meal.

Exhaustion nipped at Tess with insistent puppy teeth, the strain of having to be "on" for a while longer making her almost want to weep. She just needed a few minutes to herself away from everybody to collect her thoughts and reset. "Which way is the restroom?"

One of the other women—Liz maybe?—directed her back into the house and down the hall.

In the powder room, Tess dropped the lid of the toilet and sat, expelling a breath. She could do this. She could get through the next hour or so, make conversation, and not pass out in her plate. She could get through it without obsessing about *him*. But even as she thought it, echoes of his smile, his laugh, mocked her, and the reflection in the mirror showed her the truth she'd been trying to deny. She regretted walking away.

For half a minute, she let herself dream. Maybe she could track him down. She had wealth on her side. She could hire a private detective. Surely with a list of the places they'd stayed as they toured the Highlands, someone could find out who he really was. The innkeepers and hoteliers would've kept record of his passport. Hell, she could probably get that information herself without the detective. But then what? She'd snuck out of their bed in the dead of night, leaving nothing but a paltry note that didn't begin to convey what their time together had meant to her. Because they'd agreed to no strings. He hadn't signed on for more. So she'd left before she'd embarrassed herself by making foolish, heartfelt confessions. Before she had to watch his expression go from affection to apology—or worse, pity.

For the love of God, it's over. You ended it. You're never seeing him again. Let it go.

Impatient with herself, Tess rose and washed her hands.

This. This was why she never deviated from the plan. Because the first time she did, she fell more than halfway in love with a complete stranger.

Except he'd never felt like a stranger. From that first moment she'd seen him in the pub, he'd been familiar. Like an old friend her heart had simply been waiting to see again.

Someday this ache of loss would fade. Tess had to believe that. She'd chalk the whole thing up to a life lesson proving she simply wasn't wired for casual affairs.

Everybody was back outside. She could hear the hum of conversation through the open patio doors. Then someone laughed, and she froze, reaching for her necklace as the sound rolled over her, warming her, like a shot of honeyed whiskey.

For a few wild beats of her heart, hope flared in her chest. But she squashed it just as fast. There was no rational, reasonable way he could be here.

You are hallucinating from jet lag.

Shaking off the sensation, Tess stepped onto the patio, registering that someone else had arrived. The air began to back up in her lungs even as broad shoulders and a blond head turned in her direction and familiar, beloved hazel eyes met hers.

～

MITCH'S HEART SIMPLY STOPPED. Because Anna—*his Anna*—was standing in the doorway, looking pale with fatigue and maybe a little shock.

Impossible. How could she have found him? This had to be some kind of waking dream. He hadn't been sleeping for shit since he got home.

The vision opened her mouth and took a single step toward him before her body jerked and she pitched forward on a yelp. Mitch didn't think. He simply leapt, scooping her up before she could tumble to the flagstones. Her body—the long, slim lines of it, settled against his, warm and real.

Not a dream. She was really, truly here.

His heart exploded with fireworks and angel song and all the other ridiculous expressions of joy he'd heard people talk about and considered hyperbole. He didn't know how she was here and didn't care. The only thing that mattered was that she *was* here, and he wasn't letting this second chance pass them by.

Her hands, those perfectly-manicured hands that had explored every inch of his body, pressed against his chest. A flush crawled across her cheeks and those gorgeous brown eyes dilated as she stared up at him, breathless. His gaze dropped to her mouth and he realized it was twisted in pain. Mitch clutched her tighter. "You okay?"

"I—Jet lag and heels don't mix. I think I twisted my ankle."

Mitch tore his gaze away long enough to see what she'd tripped over. "Actually, looks like it was the sliding door track."

"Oh." She was shaking, a plea in her eyes. For what? Did she think he wouldn't forgive her for slipping out on him? Was she worried about her reception? Give him five minutes—or five hours—without an audience and he'd allay those fears.

The noise of the family all talking over each other was a roar in his ears. He didn't register much until Trey appeared at his shoulder.

"Tess, baby, are you okay?"

A flash of...something crossed her face. For anybody just glancing, they might have taken it as a wince. "I'll be fine, Dad."

Dad? Tess?

"Mitch, go set Tess down on the sofa. I'll get some ice," Aunt Sandy ordered.

Tess. As in *Trey's daughter*, Tess. The one this whole dinner was for.

Holy. Shit.

Apparently no last names had also meant no real name for her at all. As he absorbed that, Mitch registered something else. She hadn't expected to see him. She was here to visit her father. Which meant...she wasn't here for him at all. Suddenly the plea made sense. She didn't want to reveal they knew each other.

Mitch sucked in a breath, riding the wave of disappointment. Well, that was fine. He wasn't keen on explaining how he'd been intimate with the only daughter of his very protective, very *connected* new uncle. Shit. If Trey found out, Mitch might end up in a body bag, family or not.

On autopilot, he moved into the living room, his brain cycling through every moment he'd spent with this woman, analyzing and questioning everything he'd believed for the last month and change. What else hadn't been real?

Mitch settled Anna—shit—*Tess* on the sofa. Though her face had gone carefully neutral, she skimmed a hand over his arm as he pulled away. Gooseflesh rippled along his skin in its wake. He cut a glance at her, absorbing the apology of her touch and nodding once. They sure as hell needed to talk, but he'd table his assumptions and the temper that had snapped to a simmer until he had answers.

"Let's see what we've got here." He gently slipped off the heels. She hadn't worn power heels during their week together. "Which foot?"

"Left. Thanks. I'm sure playing doctor isn't quite the meeting you imagined."

Well damn if that thought didn't shoot straight to his groin. Mitch shifted to hide the erection and picked up her foot. He didn't miss the faint shiver that ran up her leg at his touch. At least she was still affected by him. "Not so much, no." As he probed the ankle, he figured two could play at this game of crosstalk. "So you mentioned jet lag. Where are you flying in from?"

"London. I've been over there the past five months."

"She's been managing some of our European concerns," Trey explained. "And doing a helluva job." Pride dripped in his tone. "She was a fifth year MBA from Yale."

Tess jerked a shoulder, looking uncomfortable. At the reveal of something real about her? Or was it something else?

"Get a chance to travel much while you were over there?"

Her gaze came back to his. "Not a lot. There wasn't much time to play."

Is that what he'd been? Just a diversion?

Mitch rotated her foot. "Does this hurt?"

"Only a little."

That made one of them.

"Probably not sprained, then." He accepted the ice pack from his aunt and draped it over Tess's ankle, holding it in place on his knee because, fool that he was, he needed to touch her, to maintain whatever tenuous thread of connection they had.

Norah came in with a tray of coffee stuff. "Better late than never. How do you take it?"

"Cream, no sugar." The answer tripped off Mitch's tongue before he could stop it. *Crap.*

Tess shot him a facsimile of her real smile. "Good guess."

"Cream, no sugar, it is then." Norah fixed the coffee and passed over the heavy stoneware mug, along with a couple of painkillers.

"Thank you. I'm sure it'll be fine with just a little ice."

Norah smiled and tugged at Mitch's arm. "Why don't you take a few minutes to absorb everything? The Campbell clan is a lot to take in all in one fell swoop, even when you're not exhausted. We'll get you when dinner is ready."

He didn't see any choice. There was no reason he could give them why he ought to stay with her, and the family would sure as shit frown at him flirting in his usual fashion. He stood to shift Tess's foot, dislodging the ice pack. They both lunged for it and Tess's hand ended up over his. For just a moment, Mitch closed his eyes, absorbing the feel of it. How many nights had he lain awake dreaming of just this?

She squeezed gently. "Would you mind keeping me company? If someone doesn't keep talking to me, I'm going to pass out, and then you won't be able to wake me for dinner."

They could hardly have the conversation they needed to have here. Not with the endless parade of his family. But he'd take any excuse he could to be near her. "Sure."

Because Mitch didn't trust himself not to give their connection away, he settled her foot on a pillow and took the next chair. A hundred questions clogged his throat, creating a logjam in the suddenly awkward silence between them. Not once had they been awkward together in Scotland. Behind them, various family members went in and out of the kitchen. He'd never really had cause before to hate that there were so damned many of them.

"So, what does a fifth year MBA from Yale do for fun? Hiking? Go to the theater? Sing karaoke?" *Pick up random men for a week long affair?*

Trey caught the tail end of the question and laughed. "Tess do karaoke? That'll be the day."

It certainly was.

Her expression was totally neutral, but he could see the discomfort beneath. "It wouldn't be my go to, no. Karaoke isn't what you call dignified, and a Peyton must always be dignified."

"So your grandmother always says," Trey agreed.

"That doesn't sound like much fun," Mitch observed.

"We have to be careful with our fun, lest it wind up in the media and reflect poorly on the company," Tess intoned.

Was that why she'd given him a totally bogus name? To keep a low profile from the media? Mitch couldn't wrap his brain around the need for that kind of discretion. It was just one more clue to exactly how little he really knew about her.

Her father bent over and kissed the top of her head. "You could never do a thing to reflect poorly on the company or the family."

An indulgent smile hovered at the corners of her mouth. "You're biased."

"I'm allowed."

"Time to turn the steaks!" someone hollered.

Trey disappeared to man the grill and the oppressive tension descended again.

"So you live in Wishful?" Tess laced her hands together in her lap, tight enough the knuckles went white.

"Yep. Born and raised. Came back after grad school. I'm an architect." These were the identifying personal details they'd carefully avoided. All the usual get to know each other stuff they'd skipped right over.

Her eyes brightened with interest and she shifted toward him, those tight-knit hands loosening. "Commercial or residential?"

"Some of both."

"And you can actually make a career at that in a place this small?"

Every cell in his body wanted to lean toward her, but he crossed his leg instead, slouching back in the chair and drumming restless fingers on the arm. "I work on projects all over the country. Some of that requires travel, but mostly I can design from anywhere, so I choose to do that from home. What about you? You're part of the family business, obviously."

"With the exception of this project I've been managing in London, I'm based in Denver."

Tap. Tap. Tap. "This your first time in Mississippi?"

"It is. I never had reason to come here before."

Tap tap. Tap tap. "I guess with your dad moving here, you'll be here again in the future?" God, he hoped he didn't sound as pathetic and desperate as he felt asking that question.

"I guess we'll have to see."

As they got called to dinner and Mitch held out a hand to help Tess up, he reflected that at least she hadn't said an outright no. He could work with that.

CHAPTER 3

*S*omehow Tess made it through dinner without falling asleep in her plate, throwing herself at Mitch to beg his forgiveness, or otherwise saying anything that revealed their intimate association. She was calling it a win. As soon as dessert was cleared, she pushed back from the table. "This was delicious, and it was wonderful to meet all of you, but I am literally dying of jet lag right now, so I'd really like to head on to the hotel."

Sandy exchanged a look with Trey. "Oh, we thought you'd stay here with us."

Even in her state of exhaustion, Tess knew she'd offended the other woman and scrambled to find something appropriate to say that would make this better. Because she couldn't stay here in this house, watching the two of them making googly eyes at each other. "I really appreciate the offer, but I have work I need to get to early in the morning, and I was just going to hijack Dad's office at The Babylon rather than disturb anybody."

Trey shoved back his own chair. "I'll drive you into town."

Mitch leaned over to grab empty dessert plates and pile them into a stack. "I can drive her. I need to head right by there on the way to my house."

Tess knew her role in this. "Oh, I wouldn't want to trouble you."

"No trouble," he said easily.

"That's very kind of you. I'd appreciate it."

Nobody fought about it, and she didn't think anybody even looked at them crossways. Which was how she found herself tucked into the front seat of Mitch's truck as he pulled away from the curb fifteen minutes later, bracing herself for the confrontation that had been building for the last two hours. She had no idea how this was going to go. She deserved whatever anger or accusations he wanted to throw her way. She'd snuck out on him like a coward in the night, after the most profound sexual experience of her life. Because it hadn't been just sex. It had been lovemaking. Intimacy at the purest level, and way the hell more than either of them had agreed to with their no strings fling. It had scared the shit out of her.

"I'm so fucking happy to see you."

His voice was full of such unmitigated joy, she snapped her head toward him. Mitch glanced at her, and even in the waning light she could see he wasn't angry. The relief of that bled through her, loosening the knots that had slowly been tightening in a noose around her heart since she walked out on that patio. Free of prying eyes, Tess shifted in her seat to drink him in. Her fingers itched to tunnel into that thick blond hair with just a little wave. The golden scruff of his five o'clock shadow darkened his jaw, and there were faint shadows beneath his eyes, as if he hadn't been resting any better than she had. His broad shoulders filled out the Oxford cloth shirt, and the muscles in his forearms stood out in stark relief against his rolled-up sleeves as he gripped the steering wheel. Even with the signs of strain, just looking at him had pleasure and joy coursing through her.

"I'm happy to see you, too. Surprised, but happy."

Mitch snorted a laugh and a dimple winked in his cheek, making her heart flip. God, she'd missed that dimple. "I don't think surprised even begins to cover it. So maybe we can start with some of the essentials we avoided in Scotland. You're Tess Peyton. Not Anna."

"Teresa Anne, actually. My mother's middle name is Anna."

"I get the no last name thing. But why give me a different first name?"

Tess blew out a breath. "Nothing about that week was something Tess Peyton could or would do. Because, as I said, all of my actions prospectively reflect back on the company. I wanted the chance to be someone else, who didn't have the burden of all those expectations. I wanted someone to look at me as *me* first and not Tess Peyton at all. And at the time, I didn't think it would matter because I hadn't planned on more than one night. And then..."

"The best laid plans," he murmured.

"Oh, I'm sure Robert Burns is having a grand laugh at my expense from beyond the grave. Because I plan *everything*. I'm always, always in control." She liked the comfort of routine and predictability. Preferred to know exactly what was happening when. It didn't take a therapist to point out that was a defense mechanism she'd developed as a kid, when her parents had divorced and she'd had no control.

"Except not with me."

"Not with you," she agreed. "And that was...freeing." Tess hadn't expected that, and maybe it had contributed to her willingness to extend that time out of time. Or maybe it had simply been the man himself.

"So is that what we were? A vacation from your real life?" His tone was neutral, casual.

What did he want her to say?

"That's how it started, yes. But I need you to know, Mitch—I may have omitted a million details, but my name is the only thing I outright lied to you about. I could see you wondering about that all through dinner. You met *me*. Not the businesswoman. Not the billionaire's daughter. Not whatever other lens people usually see me through. None of it was an act."

Unable to read his expression, Tess shifted toward him, giving in to the urge to touch him and laying a hand on his thigh. The muscles were tense, belying his easy manner.

"You disappeared on me." There was no anger in his tone, though she knew she deserved that.

Swallowing against a knot of tears, she tried to find the words. "I'm sorry. I'm so sorry. I couldn't face saying goodbye to you."

After another long moment, his hand dropped to cover hers, and the relief of that touch almost had the tears spilling over.

"I didn't want to say goodbye either."

Everything in her wanted to unbuckle her seatbelt and snuggle up to him. But there were too many unanswered questions, too much reality between them for more than this small connection. Still, she turned her hand to curl her fingers around his, basking in the warmth of his palm against hers and that soothing sense of the familiar.

He slid away as soon as they reached the hotel, and she instantly regretted the loss of his touch. Grabbing her bags out of the backseat, he ushered her inside. It was the first time Tess had been to The Babylon. The boutique hotel and spa had been a pet project of her father's, one she now knew he'd invested in as a reason to be near Sandy. But it hadn't been purely personal. She'd seen the financials on the place. It had proved to be a good business decision.

The lobby was elegantly appointed, with what felt like acres of Italian marble and a grand staircase of Cocobolo rosewood climbing to the second story. She'd seen the plans, knew there was a ballroom a little ways down the hall. The bar and dining room were at the front of the hotel, facing the expanse of the town green. Further down the block were the spa and conference facilities, but this central portion of the hotel housed two floors of high end guest rooms above the public spaces.

The woman in the navy blazer behind the front desk offered her a friendly, professional smile. "Welcome to The Babylon. How can I help you?"

"Reservation for Tess Peyton."

The desk clerk snapped to attention like a soldier at inspection. "Yes, ma'am. Miss Peyton. We have you in the penthouse suite." Her hands moved with brisk efficiency, preparing the key card. "Do you need anything? Room service? Would you like to book any spa treatments?"

A massage probably wouldn't hurt, but she'd look into that tomorrow.

"No, thank you. I'm good for now." Tess accepted the key and turned to Mitch, intending to make their awkward goodbye. But he was already heading toward the elevator. She hurried to catch up. "What are you doing?"

"Carrying your luggage."

"I can do that myself."

He spared her an amused glance. "A gentleman doesn't allow a lady to wrestle with her own luggage. Especially not when she's turned her ankle."

The ache had faded to almost nothing during dinner. She'd forgotten.

In the elevator car, she stood in the opposite corner, well aware of the security cameras. There'd be more in the hall. She didn't know how often or even if her father reviewed them, but she wasn't taking any chances at generating questions she didn't want to answer. She wasn't sure what Mitch had in mind, but she knew what was likely to happen if he followed her into her room and into the first true privacy they'd had. She'd wanted him from the moment they'd met in Scotland. That had only intensified in their weeks apart. Part of her wanted to give in to that desire. To kick the door shut and revel in this chance meeting.

But how foolish would that be? Walking away from him the first time had nearly done her in. Being with him again would only deepen what they'd already started and make their inevitable parting that much worse. His life was here. Hers was in Denver. And even if neither of those things were true, they had the complication of their new family connection. As long as her father and Sandy stayed together—and she had no reason to believe that wouldn't be permanent—Mitch was going to be in her life. Picking back up with an affair that could go nowhere would just make that all kinds of awkward in the future.

Saying nothing, she slid the keycard into the door and pushed it open.

Mitch followed her inside, setting down the suitcase and briefcase before turning toward her. His eyes searched her face, and she wondered what he was looking for, what he saw.

"I should go. You need to get some rest."

Apparently he saw the jet lag. Well, that did wonders for her ego.

His lips curved. "You're so transparent when you're tired." And at last, at long last, he stepped into her, lifting a hand to her cheek. "It doesn't mean I don't want to stay."

She didn't wrap around him the way she wanted, but she couldn't stop herself from turning into the touch. "That would be really complicated and probably a bad idea."

His eyes dilated as he looked down at her, and she knew he was thinking about all the delicious, glorious ways they could enjoy that bad idea. As erotic memories bombarded her brain, Tess's resolve began to weaken.

Mitch stroked his thumb across her cheek, lighting little fires along her skin. "We're both back in the real world. Tess Peyton's world."

That wasn't nearly the splash of cold water it needed to be. "Yeah."

"So I'm gonna go." After another long moment, he pressed a kiss to her temple. "Get some sleep, baby."

Her fingers curled into her palms to keep from grabbing onto him as he stepped away. "Thanks for your help with my bags and the ride."

"Anytime. Goodnight, Tess."

"See you around, Mitch."

Another flash of smile and he was gone, leaving her alone with her exhaustion and regrets.

~

WITH EVERY STEP away from Tess, Mitch's body tightened in resistance. All the way down the elevator and through the lobby, he wanted to go back to her, to wrap her in his arms and pretend the last weeks hadn't happened. But they were back in the real world. And hers wasn't the only one with complications. This was his hometown and he was under no illusion that if he stayed longer than a few minutes in her hotel room, it wouldn't get back to his family. And her father.

"Mitch Campbell!"

The hail had him turning toward one of the benches that had been added to Main Street as part of the facelift Norah had orchestrated downtown. A pair of familiar blue-haired ladies beamed at him. Manners dictated he walk over and speak instead of bolting like a jackrabbit.

"Evening Miss Betty, Miss Delia. Where's y'all's third Musketeer?" It was rare to have a Casserole Patrol sighting without all three of them in attendance.

On a huff, Miss Delia Watson crossed her arms over the massive handbag in her lap. "She's off for a date night with Chester. Again."

"We're feeling a mite neglected, to tell you the truth," Miss Betty admitted.

Mitch tucked his tongue in cheek. "Y'all haven't asked if Chester's got a couple of buddies?"

"Sonny, that ain't so easy at eighty as it was at your age," Miss

Delia announced. "Besides, they aren't on the kind of date night you bring company to, if you take my meaning."

He nearly choked. He could've gone the rest of his life without that kind of visual in his brain. "Fair enough. So what are you two ladies up to this fine evening?"

"We just finished dinner at Speakeasy and thought we'd take a little mosey around the green before heading home." Miss Betty batted her lashes. "Be a dear and walk us to our car?"

Well knowing his job here, Mitch resigned himself to interacting a while longer. If there was one activity the members of the Casserole Patrol enjoyed more than ogling young men, it was flirting with them. With a gallant sweep, he offered his arms to them both. On a delighted little giggle, they rose and tucked their tiny hands at his elbows.

"Which way?"

Miss Delia patted his arm. "We're parked around past the bakery."

They began to stroll.

Miss Betty tipped her face up, her sharp eyes gleaming. "Who was that lovely young lady you escorted into the hotel there?"

Proof positive that he'd done the right thing in walking away tonight. "Trey's daughter is in town for the week. She just got in from London this afternoon."

"London! My, that's exciting."

"I expect it is. We had a big family dinner to welcome her to town."

"Pretty girl," Miss Delia observed.

"Yes ma'am, she is." It was pointless to deny.

The silence stretched out, both of them obviously waiting for more. Mitch kept his mouth shut.

"Is she single?" Miss Betty prodded.

No, she's damned well not. She's mine. But no matter how he felt, that was no certainty. Either way, he wasn't about to give voice to the notion in front of these two. "It didn't come up at dinner."

Miss Delia tsked. "Falling down on your game, son. Time was you'd have had that detail inside five minutes of conversation."

She wasn't wrong, but Mitch had to repress a sigh. He knew he'd earned his reputation as a woman-loving flirt over most of his adult life, but it was starting to piss him off. Was it so hard to believe he could grow to want other things? And, okay, maybe it wasn't so much growth as a sudden realization that with the right woman, the whole prospect of marriage and family felt like the best kind of adventure instead of a prison.

Not that it mattered. "She's family now." He needed to remember that.

Miss Betty waved a hand. "Pish posh. No blood ties there. Lord knows the dating pool in this town is shallow at any age."

"Are you determined to pair off everybody who comes to town?"

"Well why not? Then Norah would have a whole new angle to play up for the tourists. We could be the Southern city of love."

Amused despite himself, Mitch decided to throw Norah to the gossip wolves in granny's clothes in hopes of getting the attention off him. "I'm sure she'd love to hear about that idea. You should let her know."

"I just might do that."

The two of them debated how to present it on the last block of their walk, and Mitch made all the appropriate encouraging noises. It kept them off his back and off the topic of his love life. Still, he was beyond grateful to spot Miss Delia's big, white Cadillac.

"Here we are, ladies. Safe and sound." Because he knew it would please them, he stooped to brush a kiss to each papery cheek. They giggled and patted his arms.

"You're a good boy, Mitch Campbell."

He waited until they were ensconced in the monster of a car and had safely backed out of the parking space before turning to cut across the green back to his own truck.

Disaster averted. For now.

But he couldn't stop thinking about what they'd said. He and Tess weren't family. Yeah, it was complicated. There were a whole lot of negative "if it doesn't work out" scenarios that would end in an awkwardness that would impact everybody. But what if they did work out? What if everything they'd felt in Scotland—away from all the bullshit and pretense that usually took months to peel away in the course of normal dating—what if that was as real as it got?

He'd been desperate for more time with her and now, here she was. For one more week, at least. Mitch knew it wouldn't be like their week abroad. They both had responsibilities and obligations that would keep them from spending every waking—and sleeping —minute together. But this was a chance to legitimately explore whether they could find a way to make their real worlds mesh. He'd be a fool to walk away from that.

Brimming with fresh purpose, Mitch shifted directions, heading straight for the fountain that was the town's namesake. Fed from nearby Hope Springs, the post-Civil War fountain was at the center of Norah's rural tourism campaign that had helped breathe new life into the town's economy. She'd capitalized on local lore that wishes made in the fountain actually came true. Mitch had half-assed some wishes over the years. Maybe that was why they'd never come true. Because he didn't put the full force of belief and desire behind them. Well, he had the desire now.

Digging a quarter out of his pocket, he clutched it tight, drawing up every iota of longing he'd felt from the moment he'd woken to find her gone. *I wish for a real chance at a real relationship with Tess. The forever kind.*

He tossed the coin, hearing the decisive splash as it hit the water. Knuckle tapping the top of the basin wall, he turned and headed home to plan.

CHAPTER 4

*J*ess woke at four in the morning feeling fluish and hung
over. Jet lag on a return trip from Europe always
kicked her ass but not usually this bad. Maybe she still had a touch
of food poisoning. Or maybe she was just emotionally wrung out
after family dinner and seeing Mitch again. She tried to drift back
to sleep and into the lovely dream she'd been having about that
rainy day they'd spent in a B and B in Inverness but recognized it
as a lost cause. For better or worse, her body thought it was ten
and well past time to get up.

Forcing herself out of bed, she pushed herself through some
yoga. Half a dozen sun salutations later, she crawled into the
shower. It was nearing five by the time she searched through the
kitchenette for a kettle. Of course there wasn't one. This was the
U.S., where coffee ruled the day. Unable to face the pod coffee on
her iffy stomach, and unwilling to suffer the indignities of pod tea
—living in the UK had turned her into a tea snob—she called
down to the front desk and requested boiling water. Room service
didn't actually open for an hour yet, but being the boss's daughter
had its perks.

While she waited, she pulled out her laptop to check on things for work. There were some final details to tend to on the Picadilly project, things she'd go over with her staff during their video conference later. After she got some caffeine in her system. Then she'd finish prepping the pitch to her father about the greater role she wanted to take in the company in Denver. It wasn't that she wanted to run things in his absence, though she'd enjoyed getting her teeth into a real challenge. But she wanted Peyton Consolidated to expand in a new direction. To not just work at building their own business but to nurture others. With the resources at their disposal, they could usher in a new wave of small businesses that would help bolster economies all over the U.S. It was a dream she'd discussed with no one except Mitch, and even then only in the most general terms. She had to prove herself capable before she brought the concept up to her father, and the Picadilly project would go a long way toward that.

One step at a time.

At the knock on the door, Tess thanked God for prompt and attentive staff.

"I really appreciate..." She trailed off because it wasn't room service at her door. "Mitch?"

"Thank God, you're awake. Can I come in?"

Tess stepped back, staring as he walked past her. "What are you *doing* here? Is something wrong?" She couldn't fathom why he'd show up at this ungodly hour if it wasn't an emergency.

"I didn't sleep last night." Restless energy rolled off him in waves as he paced a tight circuit around the room. "I was too busy thinking about you, about us. About this second chance we've been given."

"Second chance? I—"

Mitch took her hands, squeezed. "Just hear me out. There's something between us, Tess. We both wanted more in Scotland."

Her fingers clenched reflexively around his. It thrilled her to hear him confirm that, even as it terrified her.

"Maybe we didn't plan on it, but so the hell what?" With every word, he closed the distance between them. "We found each other in the big wide world, and even after we went our separate ways, against all odds, Fate threw us together again."

"In possibly the most awkward way possible," she reminded him. Because his enthusiasm, his hope, was infectious, and she couldn't risk allowing herself to believe in the fairy tale.

"It's not ideal. I get that." He cupped her face. "But I can't walk away from this. I can't walk away from you."

Even as warmth pooled in her chest, Tess reached up, intending to pull his hand away, to be the voice of reason they needed. But she curled her fingers around his wrist instead, forging another link between them. "I'm not going to be here that long. Only a week."

The dimple winked. "Look how far we got in the first one."

More than halfway in love. Her heart teetered at the edge of the precipice just looking at him, every cell of her body wanting to lean into him with a resounding, "Yes!"

In a desperate bid for sanity, she insisted, "It's not the same. It's not *just* us this time."

"So? Now's our chance to figure out if we can make our real world lives mesh. We owe it to ourselves to explore this."

Her heart began to pound with a desperate, fearful hope.

God, was that even a remote possibility? Did they have a chance in hell of finding a way to make this into something real and lasting? It terrified her how much she wanted that, how much she wanted to believe that they could make this work. If he'd been any other man, just a guy with no connection to her family, she wouldn't be hesitating. But what if it didn't work out? There was no question that it would break her heart. Could she really deal with the backlash of that every single time she came to visit her father? Was a week really enough time to figure any of this out?

Mitch stroked his thumb along her cheek, a whisper of a touch that had her turning her face into him, chasing the warmth.

"Maybe it's not as much time as we want, but it's still more. And I'll take every minute with you I can get. Don't say no, Tess."

Last night it had taken everything she had to talk herself out of this. To convince herself that keeping her distance was the responsible thing to do. But in the face of his plea—which felt a helluva lot like a declaration—she just...couldn't. If that made her weak, she didn't want to be strong. She just wanted this man in her life for however long she could have him, consequences be damned.

She closed the distance between them, lifting to slant her mouth over his. Mitch folded her into his arms, his hand slipping into her hair, even as his tongue slid into her mouth. She opened for him. His taste seeped into her, a drug she'd been too long without. Relief fueled the spark of desire, had her moaning, pressing closer, wanting more. His hand skated down her back, over her hip, tugging her against the hard ridge of his erection. Rising to her toes, she shifted her hips against him, seeking to assuage the ache between her thighs, and earned a growl in return. She needed him, needed to wipe out the time and distance between them. The knock on the door was the only thing that stopped her from dragging him back to the bedroom and picking up exactly where they'd left off in Scotland.

Mitch lifted his head, a faintly feral expression in his eyes. "Who the hell is knocking on your door at five o'clock in the morning?"

"Room service." Tess stepped away, smoothing her hair down and scrubbing a hand over her face. As if that was going to somehow wipe away the thoroughly kissed expression. "Hide. You can't be seen here at this hour. People will think you were here all night."

With a wicked grin, he disappeared into the bedroom. God, she hoped he behaved himself. If he so much as crooked a finger, she'd be tempted to fall into that bed, and she had that conference call in fifteen minutes. Struggling to put the thought out of her mind, Tess tugged open the door. After a brief exchange that included profuse thanks and an enormous tip, she carried the hot water to the kitchenette and added one of the silk teabags she'd brought with her from England.

Hands slid over her hips, drawing her back against the length of Mitch's body. He nuzzled at her neck. "You're really stopping to make tea now?"

He was still hard, the ridge of his cock nestled against her backside. Tess curled her hands around the counter as her knees went loose. "I really am. Because I...have a video conference in—" She checked her watch. "—ten minutes, and I can't...have you mussing me up any more than you already have."

"Sure?" Mitch swiveled his hips.

"Oh God," she moaned, giving in for just a moment to press back against him.

He nibbled at her ear. "I could be fast."

For a few glorious seconds she considered it. As primed and on edge as she was, it probably wouldn't take much. But she didn't need to have post-orgasmic glow or sex brain going into this meeting. Reluctantly, she stepped way. "Fast is not exactly your hallmark. Nor would I want it to be." Setting a timer for the tea, she turned. "You really probably shouldn't muss me at all here. Too many prying eyes and ears who could take it back to my father. And I don't want him to know about this. Not until we know—"

"—whether it's worth moving heaven and earth and enduring the opinions of the family for. I get that. It's gonna be an awkward situation. I'd just as soon not give your daddy reason to hire a hit man."

"Don't be absurd. My dad would not hire a hit man." She paused for effect, keeping a straight face. "He's got one on retainer."

Mitch snorted. "Oh yeah, I met Kane last year."

Amusement had the corners of her mouth kicking into a full-on smile. "He's got that Red Grant vibe minus the British, right? But really, he's not a hit man. He's ex-CIA."

"I cannot tell you how hot it is that you know your Bond movies. That aside, what Kane is is a scary son of a bitch, who I don't want coming after me because I laid a hand on his boss's only daughter. Even though I didn't know she was his daughter at the time."

She sobered. "Would it have made a difference if you had known?"

He drew her in again, lacing his hands at the small of her back and rubbing lazy circles along her spine with his thumb. "I'd have maybe not jumped quite so quick, but I don't think I could've stayed away. Because I think this pull would've been there regardless."

"Then I'm glad you didn't know. Because I wouldn't change a single thing about our week together. Except for how it ended."

"Water under the bridge, baby. We're starting a new one now."

"If we're going to make the most of it, we need a legitimate reason to spend time together that no one would suspect."

Mitch angled his head, a slow smile spreading across his face. "I've got an idea."

"Mr. Peyton will see you now."

Mitch nodded to Louis. Like the rest of the family, he'd met Trey's frighteningly efficient PA, but he'd never had cause to go through him for a formal appointment before. He hoped Tess was right about this setting the right tone for the request. He hoped a whole helluva a lot because it felt like his future was riding on this.

Hours had passed since he'd left Tess this morning to shower, shave, and make himself presentable. She'd had meetings, and she'd insisted she needed the chance to update her dad on the

London project she was wrapping up, so that he'd be suitably impressed before they made their pitch. Mitch had a hard time imagining anyone *not* being impressed with her. Particularly after he'd tossed the idea at her and watched her run with it. She and Norah had that capability in common. Mitch hoped that was another point in their favor.

As he came into the room, Trey rose from where he'd been perched on the edge of the desk. "Mitch. It was a surprise to see you on my schedule this afternoon."

He nodded at the older man, eyes automatically tracking to Tess making more tea at the sideboard before he could drag his gaze back. "Well, I had a business proposition to discuss, so I figured I'd go through the proper channels."

"Business? Color me intrigued. You want coffee or anything?"

"No sir, I'm good."

"Then have a seat." Trey gestured toward the grouping of sofa and chairs.

Mitch dropped onto one end of the sofa, hoping Tess would take up the other. He couldn't touch her, hardly dared even look at her in front of her father, but he liked knowing she was close. Clasping his hands, Mitch leaned forward and focused on Trey. "I think it's fair to say that Wishful has been something of a pet project for you. I figure a large part of that is because of Aunt Sandy, but either way, you and your company have had a significant impact on the revitalization of the town."

Trey angled his head in concession of the point.

"Now I know you and Norah have ended up focusing more on the rural tourism side of things, and that's been good. But there's more that could be done."

"What did you have in mind?"

"I think you should buy the old Heirloom Home Furnishings factory."

Trey's brows shot up. "Why?"

Mitch had intended to say something about the revitalization of what had once been a cornerstone of Wishful's economy. Instead, he thought about Miranda and the bruises that had barely faded. He hadn't even been there and yet, from secondhand accounts alone, the images of that final standoff with her kidnapper, inside the old factory, were vivid and unshakable. "Because the last thing to happen there was ugly and horrible and traumatic, and I either want to turn it into something that will benefit the town, or I want to raze it to the ground. At the risk of being accused of using family connections, you have the resources to do that."

He felt rather than saw Tess's questioning gaze. He hadn't mentioned that part to her this morning, but it was driving him as much as the desire to spend time with her.

Sympathy flashed across Trey's features. "I do. And your sentiment is understandable. But what do you propose I do with it? None of our holdings are in manufacturing."

"I think you should turn into something else entirely. It's a good space. Big and solidly built. Once the last of the machinery is pulled, it could be retrofitted and divided up, and I think it could make a fantastic small business incubator." Mitch glanced toward Tess again as she crossed with a mug. "I got the idea because of something your daughter said, and it's been kicking around in my brain ever since." No reason to mention that was longer than last night.

"A small business incubator?" Trey directed this at Tess, who lowered to the sofa with her tea.

Mitch felt the small shift of the cushions and fought not to lean toward her. But he swore he could feel the heat of her from three feet away.

"It's something I had intended to talk to you about in the future." She paused, and Mitch tried not to watch as she crossed those long legs, deliberately taking time to seemingly gather the thoughts for the speech she already had down cold. "We're in a unique position to provide the space and expertise to assist small businesses in getting off the ground. As you well know, that's harder and harder for them to do in today's economy. Innovation is a key to longevity, but a lot of businesses lose out because they just can't afford the overhead or support staff or the space to really weather *getting* to that point. We could do that. We could help build businesses that will properly support their local economies in an organic way that direct investment just doesn't. I hadn't thought about doing it here until Mitch mentioned it, but the idea has merit. We could set up something like that in Wishful on a smaller scale as a test case for something broader down the line. In the current climate of anti-monopoly sentiment, that would be not only good business but good press. Something for the non-profit arm of the company. Or venture capital, if you prefer to go that route."

Trey's lips betrayed his amusement. "You're sounding like Norah."

"As you have repeatedly mentioned, she's a smart woman. I think it could be a smart move."

Her father propped one foot on his knee. "It's a thought. Who do we have who could spearhead that kind of project?"

"Me. I'm all but finished with my role in London. I had thought to go back to Denver, but this would give me a chance to get my hands dirty with something I'm really passionate about. And it would mean I get to spend some more time here with you."

"That's enough for me right there. I've missed my girl. But business is business. Go look into it. Put together a prospectus and a business plan for how you see it playing out, and show me the numbers. Then we'll talk for real."

Mitch repressed the urge to pump his fist in victory.

Tess looked over at him. "Do you think you could get ahold of some keys to show me around the space?"

"Already got them. I thought the two of you might want to look at it this afternoon, if you have time."

Trey shoved up from his chair and circled back to his desk.

"I've got a call with Bruce in half an hour, but you go ahead. If we do this, I want to know whether it's more economically feasible to retrofit the factory or build something from the ground up. Think you can work something up by the end of the week?"

"Yes, sir."

"Good. Then we'll talk about it at family dinner on Sunday. Sandy and Cam will want to know about it, and I'm sure Norah will have ideas." He grinned. "Having the mayor, a city councilman, and the city planner in one place can be handy."

Something flickered over Tess's features, there and gone again. If Mitch hadn't been watching, he'd have missed it.

"We're having another family dinner?"

Mitch wondered what the hesitation was about.

Trey smiled. "Every week." He leaned forward to pat her knee. "I know it's weird for us, but you'll get used to it. Especially if you end up sticking around." Rising, he held a hand out to Mitch. "I look forward to seeing what the two of you come up with. And if you've got the time, while you're out, why don't you give Tess the grand tour? I was going to do it myself but I got caught up in stuff. It's probably best delivered by a local anyway."

"Sure. I'd be happy to." Keeping his expression casual, Mitch turned toward Tess. "Are you ready to go now, or do you need to do something first?"

She drained the last of the tea and set her mug on the coffee table. "Ready to roll."

He tugged open the door for her. "After you, Miss Peyton."

CHAPTER 5

*T*ess was accustomed to getting exactly what she wanted, but not without working for it. No spoiling. That had been a firm rule of her mother's after her parents had divorced. No buying of Tess's affections with expensive things. Dad had been on board with that, wanting to instill in her an understanding of the value of hard work. She'd taken that lesson to heart long ago, and she was grateful for their forethought in keeping her as normal and down-to-earth as it was possible to be under their circumstances.

But as Tess strode out of his office on the top floor of the Babylon, she could barely repress the burble of excitement. Her father had just given her most of her heart's desires—both a chance to spend time with Mitch and an opportunity to get to her passion project years before she'd expected to have the chance. It was a heady combination, one that made her nervous. She knew it wasn't a done deal. It *was* business, as he'd said. The numbers would have to prove that the concept was viable. If she failed to prove that now, it might be a decade before she got another shot.

So she simply wouldn't fail.

They slipped into Mitch's truck. As he backed out of the

parking space, he tucked her hand in his and glanced over. "I can see the wheels turning in your head. When Norah gets that look, it usually means major plans are hatching."

Tess stiffened and tugged her hand away under the guise of pulling a notebook out of her briefcase. Norah. Again. Did the woman's reach have no bounds in this town? "I keep hearing about Norah and how amazing she is."

"I can assure you all comparisons are meant as a sincere compliment."

"She seems to dazzle everyone. My father isn't easily impressed." And yet, how often had Tess heard him talk about her in the past couple of years? The city planner had obviously proven herself, and Tess couldn't shake a bit of jealousy over that.

"She's a powerhouse. Brilliant, with one of the biggest hearts of anybody I've ever met. She's been a part of my family for years —long before she married Cam." There was something in his tone. A deep affection and something else that had Tess's suspicions stirring.

"Did you ever have a thing for her?" She hoped she didn't sound as transparent as she felt.

"Oh, I fancied I did for a while. She and my sister became friends in college, and we flirted for years, but it never came to anything. We never dated, and once she met Cam, that was that." He glanced over, a rueful smile bowing his lips. "I may as well tell you—because in the way of small towns, you'll hear it eventually —I've got a reputation as something of a flirt."

She'd known that without anyone making an announcement. Nobody came off as that effortlessly charming without considerable practice. Still, she feigned shock and pressed a hand to her heart. "You don't say."

Mitch didn't rise to the bait. "I like women. I can't and won't apologize for that. But I have always been a one woman at a time kind of guy, and I haven't even looked at another woman since I first laid eyes on you."

"Not even since you came home?" She wouldn't have blamed him. They'd had an expiration date and no understanding beyond it.

"Especially since I came home. My friends even staged an intervention over it yesterday."

"An intervention? Over the fact that you're not dating?" What kind of friends were these?

"Over the fact that I don't want to. It's a first for me, and they don't know about you." He twitched those broad shoulders in a shrug.

Yeah, she hadn't told anybody about their affair either.

"I'm just saying, I'm not seeing anybody but you, and I don't want to, no matter what my reputation might suggest."

Tess understood that this was important to him and wanted to put him at ease. "I appreciate your honesty, and I'm fully in agreement on monogamy. As to the rest, I can hardly judge you for whatever adult relationships you had before me. Particularly as I have benefitted from your…cultivated expertise." Just the thought of that expertise had her flushing hot.

He laughed, that wicked smile she loved so much flashing again. "We could skip the tour, and I could reacquaint you with that expertise."

Tess crossed her legs, squeezing them together against the sudden throbbing between her thighs. The man was sin personified. "May I remind you that we have legitimate work to do? Unlike Superwoman Norah—"

"Wonder Woman."

"What?"

"Cam calls her Wonder Woman."

Of course he does. "Okay, fine. Unlike Wonder Woman Norah, I still have to prove myself."

"Why?"

Tess stared at him. "I have to work twice as hard and long to have a prayer of people believing I'm in this job because I'm actually capable rather than because of nepotism. My father can afford to give me the world. It's important to me to earn it."

"Admirable. And, I would imagine, not an attitude that's the norm among those who come from that kind of wealth."

"No. Which is why I have to work so hard in the first place. I'm not going to blow this shot."

"All right then. Work first." He nodded, clearly shifting mental gears. "So Heirloom Home Furnishings was the core of the furniture industry that was the original backbone of Wishful's economy. About two and a half years ago, they picked up stakes and moved manufacturing to Mexico. The building has been vacant ever since."

As they turned down a long drive, Tess could see the building in the distance. Mitch drove through the gates—or what was left of them. The chain link panels hung askew on their hinges, twisted as if something huge had rammed through them. He continued his history lesson on the place as they went inside, but Tess had a hard time listening. He all but vibrated with tension. Her gaze swept the cavernous space, noting the metal racks around the perimeter and some kind of heavy equipment bolted to the concrete floor. The whole place was, predictably, industrial. It wouldn't have been her first choice, but the company knew all about retrofitting and restoration. Right this second, though, she was more interested in why he seemed ready to break things.

She remembered what he'd said in her father's office. "What exactly happened here?"

Mitch paused in the midst of describing how the space could be subdivided, a muscle jumping in his jaw. "My sister was kidnapped and held hostage."

"Jesus! What happened?"

"Miranda's a doctor. She was going the extra mile to help one of her patients escape a domestic abuse situation and the husband didn't appreciate her interference. He took her from her house and beat her." His voice shook on the words, his hands balling to fists. "If Ethan—that'd be her boyfriend, our chief of police—hadn't found her as fast as he did, I have no doubt the son of a bitch would have raped and killed her. As it was, Ethan got shot during the rescue, and Harley went out in a hail of bullets. Over there."

Tess followed the jerk of his head, expecting to see bloodstains on the concrete floor. But evidently someone had been sent in to clean the place. Still, a chill crawled up her spine imagining it. She took a step closer to Mitch, wanting to do something to soothe but not knowing what. She laid a tentative hand on his arm, finding the muscles rigid as iron. "That's horrible. But...she's okay now?"

"Okay is relative. The bruises have faded and her broken nose has healed. She looks fine now, and she's back at work. But she moved in with Ethan, now that he's out of the hospital, because she can't go back in her house. And she won't even drive on this side of town yet." His nostrils flared. "I wasn't here to protect her." The admission was raw, exposing a vulnerability she hadn't expected of him.

"When was this?"

"While I was in Europe."

She blinked. "Just a few weeks ago?"

"Yeah. Nobody told me until I got home. Didn't even mention it when I called to say I was extending my trip. So while my baby sister was in a fucking hospital bed, I was—" He cut himself off, but Tess didn't need him to finish.

"With me."

"Yeah." Mitch scrubbed a hand over his face. "I should have been here. I couldn't have done anything then, but I should have been here."

"And you feel guilty that you weren't."

"Yes."

Because Miranda was family, and for Mitch—for all of the Campbells, it seemed—family was everything. It wasn't a sentiment she had experience with, but she could admire the hell out of him for it. Stepping into him, Tess wrapped her arms around his waist. No intent to seduce or arouse, just offering the comfort of touch. When he folded her in, tucking her close and pressing his cheek to her hair, she counted it a victory.

"I feel guilty that I don't—can't—regret my time with you." He pulled back to look into her eyes. "I wouldn't change that week, Tess. It's just that I see the lasting impact of this shit on Miranda, and I want to do something to make it better."

She'd known he was a generous, big-hearted man. But this was a new layer to the casual lover, one she found she liked immensely. "Then I'll help you build something better." She was surprised at how much she wanted to do that for him. "But first we have to figure out the details so you can start on some plans."

"I already have some."

"You do?" How fast did he work? Had he drawn something up since this morning?

"I've been miserable since I came home. Between guilt over not being around for all this shit and missing you, I haven't slept a helluva lot. I needed something to distract me. I remembered what we talked about in Scotland, about the small business incubator thing. And even without you here, it seemed like something that would be good for the town. So I started drawing it up. I never imagined I'd get to share it with you. You wanna go see?"

He'd begun drawing up plans for *her* passion project without even knowing who she really was. She understood a lot of it was about his sister, but he'd been thinking of her, even while they'd been apart.

She found a smile. "I'd love to."

WHEN THEY REACHED the end of the factory drive, Mitch turned in the opposite direction from town.

Tess sat up straighter. "Where are we going?"

"My place." And he was grateful for it. This wasn't the first time he'd visited Heirloom since the attack, but he was still every bit as affected, thinking about what Miranda had been through there. He needed some time to regain his equilibrium.

"I thought we were going to your office."

"I work from home. If I have client meetings, I go to them or we meet on-site."

"Oh."

At the monosyllabic answer, Mitch glanced over. "Problem?"

Her eyes met his, suddenly serious. "Definitely not."

Awareness prickled along his skin. At his place they'd finally be alone. In private. Without likelihood of interruption or nosy neighbors within sight of the house. Thank God.

Nerves crept in the closer they got. His house would be the first thing she'd seen of his design. It was a representation of him in a way his other work really wasn't. He'd designed and built it not for the life he had, but for the one that existed somewhere in a hazy future that included a wife and kids. That hypothetical family had never been more than a fuzzy vision, a thing he planned on because it's what you did when you grew up. But over these past few years, as his friends married and started their families, he'd begun to feel the emptiness of the house. It was way the hell too big for just him and instead of exciting him about the possibilities of the future, the place had made him keenly aware of what he hadn't yet achieved. Before he'd left for Europe, he'd begun to wonder if he'd ever find the right woman or if he'd end up as the favorite bachelor uncle. That had only gotten worse since he came home.

But now Tess was here, back in his world, and he was about to get a real-life glimpse of the fantasy he hadn't quite let himself imagine.

He turned into the drive, winding through a copse of trees all leafed out for spring. When they broke free of the woods and caught sight of the house, she gasped.

Two stories of river rock and timber, it sprawled along the small ridge, the hipped roof dappled from the old growth trees he'd deliberately designed around. The mass of windows glinted in the late afternoon sun and daffodils lined the walk, offering a glorious pop of color that showcased the lines of the landscaping to best advantage. Thank you, Cam.

"It's gorgeous! Your work?"

"Yeah." Mitch pulled into the garage and shut the door behind them. "Come on. I'll give you the tour."

Tess followed him into the kitchen, gratifying him by making the same sound of pleasure over the acres of counter space and the six burner Viking range that he'd coaxed from her during far more intimate activities. And that just sent his brain down a rabbit hole, imagining what it would be like to boost her up on the island and shove up that prim little pencil skirt...

Slow your roll, Campbell.

But his gaze followed her hand as she stroked it reverently over the soapstone countertops and imagined the feel of it on his body. He shifted to adjust his suddenly tight khakis.

"Dear God, the dinner parties you could host with this kitchen! I'm lusting after this range. And the counter space."

"Do you like to cook?"

"I don't get to as often as I'd like, but yeah, I do. I find it relaxing." And there was something he hadn't known about her.

"Did your mom teach you?"

"Some. Mostly it was our chef, Jean Luc." She paused, her cheeks flushing. "And I realize how that sounds. But both my parents had high-powered careers and...well...that's just how it was. But since I tended to haunt the kitchen, Jean Luc told me I might as well make myself useful."

Because he couldn't resist, he edged into her space, loving how her eyes dilated as he caged her in against the counter. "What's your favorite dish to prepare?"

"I make a hell of a coq au vin. And I've never met a pasta I didn't love. That's probably the Italian in me."

"Italian?"

"My mother is from Naples. She came to the U.S. for grad school in business. It's where she met my dad."

"Do you speak Italian?"

Tess grinned and rattled something off. The sound of it rolled over him like a caress.

"I have no idea what you just said, but that may be one of the hottest things I've ever heard."

She laughed and laid a hand against his chest. "I said yes I do and asked if you actually do this magnificent kitchen justice."

"I'm an adequate cook. Like any proper manly man, I can grill, and do whenever it's my turn to host poker night. But the only real dinner party this place has seen was the year I hosted Thanksgiving. And really, I just provided the space. Grammy, Mom, Aunt Anita, and Aunt Sandy took over. We men were banished to football."

"That seems like a tragedy. This is clearly a space designed for entertaining." She nudged him gently back and wandered through the wide entryway into the huge den, with the dining room off to one side.

"You like entertaining?"

"Love it. My parents used to host these huge fancy parties when I was little. I was supposed to be in bed, but I always snuck out of my room to watch the guests arrive in their fancy party clothes. They looked so glamorous. Like real-life royalty."

Mitch liked the mental image of a tiny Tess with her face peeking out through the spindles of a staircase. "Is it just the fancy kind of parties you like?"

"No. I like entertaining, period. Bringing together friends. Doesn't have to be huge or fancy. Just good food, good company."

He could see how it might be, with the house full of friends and family, the two of them circulating, laughing, then sharing a glance across the room that made everybody else disappear. Despite their vastly different worlds, he could see how she'd fit. In this house. In his life. He'd never brought a woman here before. Hadn't wanted to have memories with any other woman in this house, other than the one he married. That he could see her here so clearly just confirmed for him everything he felt in Scotland. But he knew that was getting ahead of things. Again. So he said nothing and continued with the tour, delighting in seeing his house through her eyes.

When they reached his home office and the plans he'd been working up, conversation turned to business again. He started with the front elevations he'd drawn by hand. He'd wanted the discipline of the details. She listened patiently as he took her through the AutoCAD drawings, asking the occasional question, making a suggestion or two as he described all the conversions and features. By the time he finished, her dark eyes sparkled.

"This is almost exactly my vision."

"I know." It's what he'd been aiming for. Bringing to life everything she'd told him.

"You were paying attention." Her smile warmed him down to his toes. And a few other places.

"I remember every word you've ever said to me."

A flash of uncertainty flickered over her features. "Why did you do this? I mean, I understand why you want to change the building for Miranda. But why turn it into this?"

Mitch weighed the truth against the likelihood it would scare her away and opted for honesty. "Because it's a good idea that fits with the revitalization efforts already going on in Wishful. And because it was a way to keep you with me."

"Mitch." Her voice was drenched with an emotion he was optimistic enough to believe was hope. "I haven't taken off the necklace you gave me." Her fingers brushed over it, drawing his attention to the lovely length of her throat.

He wanted to press a kiss to the hollow. Did she remember what the shopkeeper had said? That the thistle represented devotion?

"I like seeing it on you. Maybe that's a little caveman of me."

"I don't mind. It was a way to keep you with me, too."

It wasn't precisely the declaration he wanted, but it was an opening, a beginning. An admission that he hadn't been in this alone. He could build on that. He was very, very good at building things.

Stepping into her space, he ran a finger over the silver filigree, watching her shiver, her eyes going to half mast. "I've got this fantasy about this necklace."

"What's that?" The huskiness in her tone had more blood draining out of his head.

"Seeing you wearing nothing but this, while stretched out on my bed."

She snapped her gaze to his, eyes molten.

"Will you give me that fantasy, Tess?"

Without hesitation, she stepped into him. "Yes."

Mitch cupped her nape, tipping her face up to his. But instead of taking her mouth, instead of diving headlong into the heat bubbling between them, he brushed his lips over her brow, her temple. Tiny, whispering kisses all over her face and down the column of her throat. Tess dug her hands into his waist, hanging on as he made it to the hollow of her throat and drained the starch out of her knees.

Sighing his name, she dropped her head back to give him better access. She felt his smile against her throat.

"So lovely," he murmured.

Tess wanted to strip him down as he did the same to her, until they could give in to the frenzied, frantic beat of attraction she'd felt since the moment she'd seen him again. Right here. Right now. She wondered exactly how sturdy his drafting table was. But that was her fantasy, not his, and she'd promised. So she held on and endured his ruthless patience, letting him seduce her with his touch, his kisses, into believing they had all the time in the world. She fell into that fantasy with him, in this place that was utterly his, as she wanted to be.

He eased them down the hall, never stopping his onslaught against her senses. Her jacket fell to the floor somewhere outside his home office. Gooseflesh pebbled her arms as she wondered when he'd get to her camisole. As they made it to the stairs, he slid his broad palms beneath the hem of her skirt.

"I like the power suit," he breathed.

"Yeah?"

"I'll like it better like this." He nudged the fabric up around her hips, exposing the lacy underwear. "Mmm."

Tess half expected him to drop to his knees and explore, right there. Instead, he ran his hands over her butt and down her thighs, boosting her up.

"Wrap your legs around me."

She didn't have to be told twice. Taking advantage of her position, she made her own leisurely exploration of his throat and ears as they climbed. Her nails lightly scraped along the fine hair at his nape as she very gently bit the lobe of his ear. He hissed in a breath and she abruptly found herself pinned against the wall on the landing, the hardness behind his fly pressed against her center.

"Do you know what you do to me?" he demanded.

Her lips curved into a wicked smile as she rolled her hips against him. "I have some idea."

His fingers curled into her thighs as he clearly struggled for control. "Later," he breathed. "Later I will happily take you on every surface in this house. But this first time, I want you in my bed."

"I'm holding you to that promise."

He was growling as he surged up the last of the stairs and stumbled down the hall, into a bedroom. Tess had dim impressions of heavy wood furniture and cool gray walls, before he set her back on her feet and took her mouth, his hands plunging into her hair. Tess yanked his shirt free, fingers fighting with the buttons to get to skin. The more desperate she got, the more he seemed to find his control, until they were back to that impossibly languorous pace. How could he do this, when she felt ready to fly apart at the barest of touches? Why wouldn't he let her?

When at last he'd stripped her down to the necklace and laid her back on the bed in the pool of late afternoon sun, the look on his face nearly sent her over the edge.

"You are so damned beautiful."

"Touch me."

"Oh, darlin', believe me, I intend to touch and taste every inch."

And he did. With excruciating patience, he worshipped her body, driving her up with his hands and his tongue until she screamed—twice. Only then, when she lay boneless from pleasure and the afternoon shadows had grown long, did he strip out of his own clothes and reach for a condom to sheath himself. As he crawled onto the bed, stretching out above her, Tess found the energy to lift her arms and reach for him. He settled into the cradle of her hips, finally, *finally* notching his erection into her drenched and swollen folds.

"Please," she whispered, brushing a kiss over his jaw. "Please, I need you."

Gaze fixed firmly on hers, Mitch slowly slid inside her. Waves of pleasure threatened to drag her under, and Tess had to fight to keep her eyes open. But she wanted to see him, wanted that connection as he filled her. Over the past weeks, she'd tried to tell herself she'd romanticized what she'd experienced with him.

She'd tried to convince herself that she'd attributed more to it than had really been there. But as he began to move, a torturous, delicious rhythm she hoped he could keep up until the end of time, Tess knew she'd been wrong. Because this was better than she remembered. This was more. This was home.

I love you.

The words clogged in her throat, held back only by a vague sense of panic. It was too much, too soon. She couldn't say it. Not here in his bed as he made the sweetest love to her. So she said his name instead, letting everything she felt spill out in her tone, in the touch of her hands and the rise and fall of her body as it met his. And when he lost that exquisite patience at last, when his hips began to piston faster, harder, deeper, she gloried in every stroke, clinging to him as her only anchor in the storm that washed them both away and praying that, in the end, they wound up in the same place.

CHAPTER 6

*M*itch was going to go mad if he couldn't touch Tess. That silky fall of hair shone like mink in the morning light, and his fingers itched to stroke through it. He knew perfectly well he couldn't lay a hand on her at all here. He had to police every gesture, every expression to avoid the gossip. Dinner Belles was packed full of the morning rush crowd—downtown business owners, parents who'd opted for a cup of coffee after the school drop-off, and the senior contingent who liked to meet for breakfast and linger for hours.

Tess had walked across the green from The Babylon to meet him for the tour they hadn't gotten around to for the past couple of days. They'd been far too busy having that sexy tour of his house between all the work putting together the proposal for her father. For all he'd never brought a woman there before, he would never look at any room in it ever again without imagining her naked. And he wasn't entirely sure he'd ever be able to work at that drafting table again without getting hard. The only thing that would have made it better was being able to keep her in his bed at night instead of delivering her back to the hotel after what felt like stolen hours. But they were being very conscious of appearances. So, despite the threat to his sanity, Mitch kept his hands to himself.

"What sounds good?"

She looked up from the menu and shot him an easy smile that had him wanting to loose a mile-wide grin in return. "I have no idea. It all looks amazing. What's your favorite?"

"Biscuits and gravy."

"What's that like?"

Mitch stared at her. "You've never had biscuits and gravy? Woman, what kind of sad, sheltered life have you led?"

"One outside the South."

"Your daddy's from Memphis!"

"He's been gone from Memphis a long time, and my Grandmother Peyton is not the type to indulge in home cooking."

"That's just tragic."

His horror just seemed to amuse her.

"What's got your boxers in a knot this morning?" Mama Pearl automatically refilled his coffee cup without looking.

"This poor girl has never had biscuits and gravy."

"That right?" She turned to study Tess with those unfathomable black eyes, so Mitch took it upon himself to make introductions.

"Tess, I'd like you to meet the love of my life, Mama Pearl Buckley. She makes the best pie in a three hundred mile radius. Mama Pearl, this is Tess Peyton, Trey's daughter."

"Is it now?" Mama Pearl's interest sharpened. She cut a glance back at Mitch that had him wanting to shrink down in the booth. Surely she hadn't figured out that Tess was The One.

Her *hmph* seemed to indicate otherwise as she shifted her attention to Tess. "Well now, it's nice to finally meet you. Your daddy talks about you all the time."

"Nice to meet you. Mitch informs me I have led a sad and sheltered existence and I must have a proper Southern breakfast. What do you recommend?"

Mama Pearl narrowed her eyes in speculation. "For you? Sausage biscuits and grits. You want any eggs with that?"

"Just one. Scrambled." Tess tucked the menu back between the napkin dispenser and condiment rack.

"Comin' right up."

As Mama Pearl ambled away, Tess frowned. "Isn't she going to take your order?"

"She already knows my order. And she'll remember yours until the end of time, unless you change it. It's part of her magic."

"Hey you two." Cam stopped by their table, his fingers laced with Norah's.

"It's jumping in here this morning. Do y'all mind if we join you?" she asked.

In answer, Mitch scooted over, repressing a soft sigh of relief. Much as he wanted Tess all to himself, it would be easier to maintain their cover as just friends with company there to distract the conversation. After a moment's hesitation, Tess did the same.

Cam slid in beside her. "What are y'all up to?"

"Breakfast before a proper tour of town," Mitch explained.

Norah clasped her hands in glee. "Oh, I hope you're doing a walking tour. It's the best way to see downtown and the weather's so nice."

Mitch grinned at her. "You just want me to show off your handiwork."

She grinned back. "True story. It was damned good handiwork."

"And none of us have forgotten it, Wonder Woman." Cam snagged his wife's hand and leaned across the table to kiss it.

Tess didn't quite manage to hide her wistful look. Mitch vowed to shower her with easy affection at the earliest opportunity. He wondered how long it would be before they could come clean and just be together publicly.

Cam caught Mama Pearl's eye and signaled for coffee, but it

wasn't the diner's proprietress who came over with the coffee pot, it was Delia Watson, with the rest of the Casserole Patrol in tow.

"Good morning, y'all," she said cheerily.

"Are you moonlighting as a waitress now, Miss Delia?" Mitch asked.

"Oh, Pearl's got her hands full for the moment, and I can pour coffee as well as anybody else."

Meaning she'd absconded with the coffee pot to try to get a leg up on the morning's gossip, and Mama Pearl was secure enough in her position as Queen of Gossip to let her.

"Morning Miss Betty, Miss Maudie Bell," Cam murmured, turning over his coffee cup and watching as Miss Delia filled it with only a little splash.

"Well, are you going to introduce us to your new friend, young man?" Miss Maudie Bell demanded, with a significant look from Mitch to Tess.

Miss Betty whacked her on the arm. "You'd know who it was already if you'd come out with us last week. That there is Trey Peyton's daughter, Tess."

Tess's mouth dropped open. "I feel certain I'd remember having met you."

"Oh no, dear, we haven't been formally introduced," Miss Delia cooed. "We ran into Mitch the other night after he dropped you off at the hotel."

As if that explained everything. Which, to the Casserole Patrol, it did.

Rather than launching into proper introductions, Miss Delia turned to Cam and Norah and beamed. "Now when are you two lovebirds gonna give us an excuse to start knitting those baby booties?"

Across the table, Tess choked a little on her coffee.

"Yes!" Miss Maudie Bell exclaimed. "You know we've gotta know what color yarn to buy."

Miss Betty scoffed. "I already finished my blanket. I'm just waiting for a nursery to put it in." She fixed Norah with an expectant look.

"They might appreciate a chance to just enjoy being married for a while before they start adding babies to the mix," Tess pointed out. "Statistically, marriages that wait to have children last longer."

The Casserole Patrol blinked at her as if that was the most radical suggestion they'd ever heard.

Before one of them said something like, "Why, dear?", which would no doubt be followed up by a very stiff and polite explanation of how other people's reproductive choices were no business of theirs, Mitch intervened. "Miss Maudie Bell, how are things going with Chester?"

That query sufficiently derailed the questioning, and when Mama Pearl arrived a few minutes later with a tray full of food—including Cam and Norah's usuals—the trio of nosy blue hairs headed across the diner to bug Ben Rawlings, the fire chief, about when exactly he was going to organize a fireman's calendar.

As soon as they were out of earshot, Tess muttered, "They have absolutely no right to poke at you about children."

"No, but something like right will never stop the Casserole Patrol from butting in. They mean well," Norah explained.

"But what if you didn't want children?"

"Oh, we do. Eventually. But we'd rather have a while to...practice first." Cam's smile spread slow as honey as he stroked a thumb across the back of his wife's hand.

"Yeah, yeah. Rub in your newlywed bliss, Cuz." Mitch gave an exaggerated roll of his eyes.

Norah leaned in to bump his shoulder. "Buck up. You'll find the right girl one of these days."

I will not look at Tess. I will not look at Tess.

"Anyway, we're having a cookout on Friday night. You have to come," Cam told Tess. "Everybody wants to meet you."

She paused, a spoonful of grits halfway to her mouth. "Everybody? I thought I already met everybody."

"You met the family," Norah explained. "This is all our friends."

Tess's expression was caught somewhere between a smile and a frown. "Why would they want to meet me?"

Mitch couldn't stop himself from smiling. "Honey, you're big news in town right now."

She looked a little green at that.

"Don't worry. I'll take you and run interference as necessary," he promised.

"I'd appreciate it. Can I borrow your kitchen?"

"Any time. Why?"

"Because I may not be Southern, but even I know you don't show up to a cookout empty-handed."

FRIDAY NIGHT and all its attendant socializing came way too soon for Tess's taste. But she'd dutifully prepared her appetizer and climbed in Mitch's truck for the drive, despite fantasies of bailing and making use of that gigantic soaker tub in his master bathroom.

"Cam and Norah's place is out on Hope Springs."

She glanced at Mitch over in the driver's seat. "It's really called Hope Springs?"

"Really is. The fountain on the green is fed from there. It's the whole crux of Norah's rural tourism campaign."

"Wishful, where hope springs eternal. I saw the banners." They fluttered on all the lamp posts on Main Street.

"A couple years back, GrandGoods was trying to buy up the land out here to put up one of their big box stores. That's how Norah and Cam got together in the first place. She stuck around to fight it and ended up buying the whole parcel for sale right out from under them. Then she wound up donating a big chunk of the land to the city for a park that Cam designed."

Wonder Woman, indeed. "That was incredibly generous of her."

"I think she was as much in love with Wishful as she was with Cam. Anyway, they built a house right down by the water. It's a helluva spot. If we've got time after we leave, I'll swing you by the park so you can see it."

Clutching the tray of appetizers she'd made, Tess wondered how long they had to stay to meet social obligation. She'd spent most of the day working with her father at his office, which was great, as she felt more on even keel with him when talking business. But it had meant no time alone with Mitch other than the brief stretch in his kitchen while she'd been making the bruschetta. She was hyperaware of the fact that her time here could be coming to an end. If her father didn't go for the pitch she'd put together for this small business incubator, she'd be headed back to Denver to her normal job. But that was a worry for Sunday, when they had that family dinner. For tonight, she needed to get her head in the game and be properly social. Even if all she really wanted to do was be anti-social with the man sitting beside her.

As soon as they pulled up to the house, Tess recognized Mitch's work. It wasn't the same style as his own house, but there was something in the lines of the single-story plantation home that reminded her of him.

"You designed this."

He glanced over, brows arched. "Yeah, I did."

"It's beautiful." The wrap-around porch offered stunning views of the lake beyond.

"It's suits them. Which is half the fun of the job." Parking behind the long string of cars in the drive, he reached over to squeeze her hand. "You ready for this?"

"As I'll ever be."

The sound of music and voices carried as soon as they got out of the truck. Tess clutched her tray like a shield as he escorted her to the house. Instead of going to the front door, he led her around back to where people milled around a lush courtyard that overlooked the lake. She recognized Cecily and Reed, and Cam was manning a massive grill in the outdoor kitchen, but everybody else was new to her. Greetings rang out as they approached, and Tess couldn't stop herself from hesitating. Would they be able to tell she and Mitch weren't just acquaintances? Was there a neon sign over their heads proclaiming them lovers? These were his friends and family, a huge part of those real lives they were trying to merge. What if they didn't like her?

Mitch's hand pressed to the small of her back. "It's gonna be fine."

Putting on her game face, Tess smiled and nodded as he introduced her to Tucker McGee and his fiancée Corinne Dawson; Liam Montgomery and his fiancée Riley Gower; Judd Hamilton and his very pregnant wife, Autumn; Piper and Myles Stewart, who had their infant daughter, Parker, in tow; and Tyler and Brody Jensen. The theme of the night seemed to be Happy Couple, Happy Couple. Brody, at least, was a name familiar to her. He'd been a project coordinator for Peyton Consolidated for years before coming back to Wishful. Tess had never met him, but she knew his work and knew her father held him in high esteem.

By the time they stepped into the kitchen, her head was spinning.

Norah turned from the counter and hurried around to give Tess a side hug. "Hey! Welcome! What have we here?"

"Roasted red pepper bruschetta with goat cheese. I've got all the components, but I didn't want to assemble until I got here so the crostini wouldn't get soggy. Where should I set up?"

"Right over here." She ushered Tess to a clear spot at one of the counters. "Sorry about all the people. I know there are a lot of us."

"I noticed. And let me get this straight. Mitch and I are the only not married, not engaged people here?"

Norah considered. "Well Miranda and Ethan haven't made it yet and they aren't engaged, but that's really probably only a matter of time. So...yeah I guess so."

"Okay, seriously, what do you put in the water here?"

Mitch laughed, and Tess wished they didn't have to hide their own involvement.

Norah's mouth quirked. "It's funny you should mention that. The Casserole Patrol are on me to do a campaign alleging the fountain has matchmaking powers."

"Ah, that may be my fault," Mitch admitted. "It came up last week, and I needed to redirect the conversation."

"Thanks for throwing me under the bus."

"It was done with love."

The easy affection among this group fascinated Tess. It spoke of comfort and long familiarity. She had friends, certainly, but she'd been so focused on work, on proving herself worthy of her position in the company, she hadn't taken the time to build these kinds of connections. As she assembled her appetizer and listened to the two of them tease each other, she began to yearn for something beyond Mitch himself. There was just something about this town, these people, that was unaccountably appealing. She was starting to understand what had drawn her father here other than his wife.

The door to the backyard opened, and Piper came in. The baby in her arms gave a miserable wail. "Oh my Lord, sorry, y'all. She was fine until a few minutes ago. She's been fed and changed."

"Maybe she wants a nap?" Norah suggested.

"Nah, this one isn't interested in napping. She's too awake for that." Mitch reached out to tickle the baby's cheek.

The moment those big, blue eyes locked on his, Parker stopped fussing and reached chubby hands toward him. Then, as if he'd done it a thousand times before, he simply plucked her from her mother's arms and settled her against his chest. "Hey there, big girl." He began to sway with her to the slow country song playing on the sound system. Parker made a happy burble and flailed her arms before grabbing onto the finger he offered and beaming up at him. "You just wanted to dance, didn't you?"

Tess's heart gave an unexpected, gooey thud. She wasn't a baby person and absolutely didn't understand the women she'd met who'd been as intent on starting a family as she was to advance her career. But the sight of this big, sweet man dancing with a baby made her ovaries squeeze. It was almost, *almost* enough to have her imagining a different sort of life than the one she'd been busting her ass for.

He caught her staring. "What?"

Shaking off the thought as ridiculous, Tess shrugged. "I just didn't expect you to be a baby fan."

Piper laughed. "Mitch can charm women of all ages, whether they're eight weeks or eighty."

This seemed undoubtedly true, as Parker appeared utterly besotted.

I know how you feel kid. I know exactly how you feel.

Myles came inside. "She settle down?"

"Apparently she just wanted to flirt with Mitch," Piper said. "You may have competition as her number one guy."

"Never gonna happen." As if to prove his point, Parker turned her head toward the sound of his voice and waved her arms. "That's my girl." Smoothly, he shifted the baby from Mitch's arms into his own, where she snuggled in, content.

A flicker of something that might have been disappointment flickered over Mitch's face. But he covered it with mock affront. "I'm wounded, Parker. I thought I was the only one for you."

Piper shook her head. "Daddy's girl for sure." But there was such love under the chagrin as she looked at her family.

"How old is she?" Tess asked.

"Three and a half months. I swear, she's the best oops ever."

"She wasn't planned?"

"Good gracious no. We'd been married like five minutes, and a baby this soon was so not our intention. But the Universe had other plans." Piper leaned in to kiss her daughter's cheeks. "Yes it did!"

Not knowing what else to say, Tess bit into one of the crostini. She was way outside her milieu right now and didn't want to inadvertently stick her foot in it. As a staunch career woman, she absolutely couldn't imagine that kind of an oops being a good thing. It was awesome that Piper and Myles had made the best of the situation, and clearly they doted on each other and their baby. But Tess doubted that she or anybody among her circle of friends would respond so positively to that kind of bomb. Still, watching them together set up a funny little ache in her chest.

She'd never thought much about kids and family. Marriage was something way out on the horizon. Kids were even further past that. She had goals, and she'd been on the fast track to meet them from the moment she graduated Yale with her MBA. There hadn't been anybody she'd even momentarily considered a candidate for a husband. Truthfully, she'd thought maybe she was too much like her father for marriage.

But it seemed she'd been wrong about her dad. Maybe she was wrong about herself. Her gaze swung to Mitch. As he met her eyes from across the room, she thought maybe, just maybe, for the first time in her life, something was more important than her career. Which meant she'd better nail this proposal so she and Mitch got the chance to find out.

CHAPTER 7

"*D*oes this sauce smell off to you?"

When Tess held up the spoon, Mitch obligingly took a sniff. "It smells heavenly." He started to lean in to sniff her, but she screwed up her face in a frown, attention back on the sauce.

"Something's not right." She put the spoon in her mouth, considering. "Too much garlic? Or maybe I need a touch more anchovy paste." Grabbing a fresh spoon from the drawer, she scooped up more sauce, blew on it gently, and offered it to him. "Here, you taste."

Tasting pasta sauce should not be this sexy. Mitch wondered if she realized how charmingly domestic she looked, fussing over an enormous meal in his kitchen. Did it make him a chauvinist if he imagined her with a little apron on to complete the picture? And maybe those power heels and nothing else?

"Delicious."

She still didn't seem quite satisfied, fluttering her hands in frustration. "Agggh."

He snagged her neatly around the waist, lacing his fingers at the small of her back. "Baby, relax. It's gonna be fine."

"This needs to be perfect."

"My family is many things, but perfect isn't one of them. Are you more nervous about the presentation or about cooking for all of them?"

He'd known she was anxious about the family dinner. He got it. The Campbell clan was...a lot. Especially for somebody who'd been an only child. Remembering what she'd said about cooking relaxing her, he'd made a bid to be host this week, so everybody was coming here. Tess had jumped at the idea of cooking and had, as far as he could tell, pulled out almost every pot, pan, dish, and cooking implement he owned—which, okay, wasn't as much as a kitchen like his would suggest. She'd drafted him to wash and chop and be general gopher, while she made use of the food processor he'd never even taken out of the box to create the filling that was going into the little pockets of pasta she'd made from scratch. They'd worked easily together, laughing, talking. But the closer time came to the actual dinner, the more wound up she got.

"I'm not nervous."

"Really? Because you look a little green." She was, as his grand-mother was apt to say, looking a little peaked.

"I still feel a little off from the jet lag. And I'm worried about getting everything ready at once. It's been ages since I attempted anything so complex." Patting his chest, she shoved back and went to check on the bread in the oven. "As to the presentation, I'd feel better about doing this in a boardroom instead of a dining room."

"Do you want me to set up a projector with a PowerPoint on the wall?" He said it as a joke. The flicker of hope across her face had him laughing.

The doorbell rang.

"Damn it." Her fingers briefly strangled a kitchen towel, her lips pressing into a thin line.

"They're going to love it." To emphasize the point, and because he knew he couldn't touch her for the next few hours, Mitch kissed her one last time. A soft, lingering kiss that would, hopefully distract her from the nerves and tide him over until the hordes had departed. Tess's eyes were glazed and her cheeks prettily pinked when he pulled back, her hand resting against his chest, over his pounding heart. Mitch lifted that hand to brush another kiss over her knuckles. "I'm gonna go let in the starving masses."

They'd apparently caravanned out because everybody was piled on his front stoop. As soon as he'd opened the front door, they were pushing past him, talking and laughing at once, headed straight for the kitchen. Mitch hoped Tess was ready for them.

"Holy crap, man, your house smells fantastic," Reed said.

"Smells like someone finally took advantage of the cook's kitchen you built," Cam observed.

"Wasn't me. This is all Tess." Mitch edged his way past them to begin taking drink orders.

"I think I had a foodgasm just from walking in the door," Miranda announced.

"Is it too early to hope there are leftovers?" Ethan asked.

At the stove, Tess seemed to have regained her composure. Her cheeks were still flushed, but maybe they'd think it was from the steam. "I hope you all like it. Mitch was kind enough to let me co-opt his kitchen and conscript him as sous chef."

"It's about time somebody put my son's kitchen to good use. Hey, baby." Liz wrapped an arm around him and tugged him down for a noisy kiss.

"He told me how little he cooks. I told him that was a crime in a kitchen like this." With chef-like efficiency, Tess removed the stuffed pasta pouches she'd informed him were *not* ravioli from the water and slid the next batch in.

Trey brought up the rear, setting down a few bottles of wine before circling around to hug her. "You made agnolotti!"

"Your favorite."

"I haven't had this since…"

"Mom." Tess didn't look at him as she continued bustling around the kitchen, pulling fresh bread from the oven.

Maybe her discomfort with his family had less to do with the size and more to do with her conflicting feelings about her father's marriage to Sandy. Mitch hadn't asked her what she thought about it. They'd been far too busy with other things this week. But perhaps she wasn't as delighted about it as the rest of them were.

"Mitch, you want to get the salad and *antipasti* out of the fridge?"

Shaking out of his thoughts, he hopped to follow orders. "Yes, ma'am. Am I allowed to touch it now without getting my hand slapped?"

Expression serious, she went brows up and made an eyes-on-you gesture with her fingers. "To. The. Table."

"Okay, okay. Slavedriver." Catching the quirk of her smile, he called it a victory.

Cam fell into automatic helper mode, taking the platters as Mitch passed them out of the fridge. They carried all of it into the dining room, where his cousin pinned him with a hairy eyeball.

"Dude, really?"

"What?" Mitch reviewed everything he'd said and done since the family arrived and came up with nothing untoward.

"Just, no."

"I have no idea what you're talking about." He made an unhurried retreat back to the kitchen, feeling Cam's eyes on him the whole way.

Ten minutes later, the entire crew was seated around the long, dining room table. Mitch took one end and Tess the other. Everybody fell on the food, with immediate compliments all around.

"Tess made the pasta herself," Mitch told them.

"Seriously? That's amazing. Where did you learn to do that?" Uncle Jimmy asked.

Tess darted a look at Sandy before bringing her focus back to

Jimmy. "From my mother and my nonna. I'm half Italian, so it's kind of a family requirement."

"What a delightful family heritage," Aunt Sandy said. "Mom's been teaching us all the family recipes the past few years, too."

"Except the secret to her chocolate pie," Miranda groused. "You won't let go of that one."

"A woman's entitled to her secrets," Grammy insisted.

"Speaking of secrets," Tess began.

Mitch paused, his fork halfway to his mouth. Had she decided to tell everybody about them?

"I had ulterior motives for getting Mitch to round you all up tonight. He's been helping me put together a proposal for starting a small business incubator here in Wishful."

That got everyone's attention. Tess launched into the pitch, relaxing as she warmed to her topic. "Incubators aren't anything new. They've been around since the 70s and 80s. But most of the top ones in the U.S. are industry specific. They're certainly more common in more urban areas or under the auspices of universities. But we can help foster an entrepreneurial economy here in Wishful and beyond, encouraging diversification, not only among types of business but in business owners—providing mentorship and assistance for groups historically disadvantaged in the business world, like women or people of color."

She'd been thorough, and it showed in her ready ability to answer the questions tossed out by her father, Aunt Sandy, Norah, and Cam.

"I actually have copies of the proposal put together, including an indexed list of all the vendor quotes, a compare and contrast between conversion of the existing space, and bulldozing and starting from scratch, with pro and con lists for both, as well as copies of the plans Mitch has drawn up for both. He talked me out of putting one at each place setting."

Cam grinned. "Are they color-coded?"

Tess looked at him like he was an idiot. "Of course."

Norah clapped her hands on a laugh. "Oh, Tess, you are my people."

They launched into further animated discussion, and Tess lost that air of discomfort she'd had since everyone arrived.

Miranda leaned in. "What are you smiling about?"

"Just thinking there's an extraordinary amount of devastatingly attractive brain power at this table."

His sister rolled her eyes. At the opposite end of the table, Tess apparently caught his words because she smiled.

Miranda lowered her voice and leaned closer. "What are you doing, big brother?"

Mitch sobered and shifted his attention. "Trying to wipe your bad memories off the face of the earth."

For a fleeting moment, her expression softened. "I appreciate it. But that's not what I'm talking about."

Yeah he knew that. "I'm not doing anything."

"Keep it that way."

He fought not to bristle, not to react at all. He'd known the family wouldn't approve of his involvement with Tess. But he hadn't expected them to keep warning him off when they didn't even know something was going on. Damn it, he and Tess had something together, and they deserved the chance to see what it was.

"I'll want to see the plans and look over the final numbers, but as far as I'm concerned, the project is a go," Trey announced.

Tess pulled out her planner. Where the hell had she been hiding that during the meal? "This puts me here for...at least four months. Maybe six, depending on the contractor's schedule once we get that hammered out." She marked something on the calendar, and as she flipped to a fresh page, Mitch resisted the urge to whoop. "I'll need somewhere else to stay. I've already checked, and the penthouse suite has another booking in three days."

"We'd love to have you stay with us," Sandy said.

Tess's smile was a little too stiff. "That's, um—"

"But I'm sure you'd rather have your own space," Sandy finished.

Some of the tension went out of Tess's shoulders.

Trey grabbed another piece of bread from the basket. "The Babylon should have something for you."

"For this length of time, I'd much rather have someplace to spread out."

She didn't look at him, but Mitch knew she was considering the issue of privacy. He was too busy thinking about an entirely different means of spreading out.

"—and a kitchen. I need a really good kitchen. And a proper office. There's not really room for me in yours at The Babylon. I need my own space, my own files, my own project board." She scribbled in the planner, probably adding to her list.

"Mitch designs killer offices," Cecily announced. "You should see what he helped turn the old train depot into for me."

"That was a fun project. And yeah, I could work something up for you, once you settle on a space." He was already turning over concepts in his mind, thinking about what he'd learned about how she worked over the past week.

"I don't know that I'm ready to actually buy and renovate something. That seems an unnecessary expense until I know I'm here for the long haul. Honestly, I'll take a lot of my meetings on-site, so it's just a work space for me. Probably best to keep things all in one place. My stuff is split between Denver and London right now. Does anybody do fully-furnished rentals in town?"

"What about here?" Grammy asked.

"Say what now?" Mitch stammered.

"You've got this gigantic house, and you're just rattling around in it alone."

"Oh, I couldn't impose—" Tess began.

"Nonsense. We're all family now, and family helps out."

"Helen, I'm not sure that's the best—"

Grammy cut Trey off. "It's a fine idea. Tess is a good girl. She can rub off on our Mitch."

That sent his brain down yet another highly inappropriate path. "I'm sorry?"

Liz pursed her lips in consideration. "Helen might have a point. With Tess here, it'll keep you from shoving two weeks of dirty laundry in the hall closet five minutes before family dinner."

Mitch felt the back of his neck heat. "Mom! You went into my closet?"

"I was just looking."

For what?

"It could be a good thing." Reed grinned. "She could tell us about all the women you're 'not dating.'"

He opened his mouth to insist he didn't bring women here, then promptly closed it again. That would make it sound like he took them somewhere else, and he wasn't doing *that* either.

"Or teach him to cook for the ones that he does," Uncle Jimmy mused, tongue tucked firmly in cheek.

"It would certainly streamline planning for the incubator to both be in the same workspace," Norah added. "And don't you have that second office in the guest suite upstairs?"

Mitch shot her a look, wondering what the hell she was up to. "Well, yes."

"See there?" Grammy said. "All joking aside, Tess isn't ready to buy something and probably doesn't want to be locked into any kind of a lease until her plans are more firmly settled. This is the ideal solution until she makes up her mind. Office and living space in one."

Don't look too eager. He shifted his attention to Tess, doing everything in his power to keep his expression dialed to I'm-just-humoring-my-grandmother. She looked a little like she'd been flattened by a steam roller. "You *are* in love with my kitchen."

"Any food-loving person with a pulse would be in love with

your kitchen. Is this your bid for me to move in and take over cooking duties?"

"You can hardly blame a guy for dreaming after this meal. But only if you want to. Either way, you're more than welcome. I'm not using the space." He could see she was overwhelmed.

"I'm not sure this arrangement is...appropriate." Trey's face was set in the kind of careful expression Mitch bet he used in sensitive negotiations. He could only imagine what was going through the other man's mind.

Grammy cocked her head, all innocence. "Why's that, Trey? His issues with laundry aside, I know my grandson was raised to be a good host and a gentleman."

A muscle jumped in Trey's jaw and they all waited to see if he'd say what he was really thinking—that he was worried Mitch would debauch his daughter.

Way too late for that.

In the end, Trey said nothing, and Mitch struggled not to let his sigh of relief rush out in a gush.

Tess finally lifted her eyes to his. "If you're sure I wouldn't be in the way—"

"That's the spirit! Easy as pie. And this way Tess won't feel like she's cramping the newlyweds' style." Grammy nodded and tossed down her napkin, clearly signaling an end to the discussion. "Now, speaking of pie, is there dessert, dear?"

SOMEHOW, Tess made it through dessert and the viewing of Mitch's plans with nobody calling her out for acting anything other than normal. Not that anybody here, including her father, really knew what normal was for her. The family insisted on utilizing their small army status to wipe out all the dinner dishes, and she could hardly protest on the grounds of needing the time and space to have a little freak out. So she said thank you instead and chatted over a cup of tea as they made short work of the mess she'd made.

"Sandy and I can drive you back to the hotel."

"I appreciate that Dad, but I think Mitch and I need to iron out the details here." Like whether they were really going through with it.

Her father looked like he wanted to say something else, but bit it back. "You'll be needing a car."

"I expect I will. I'll add it to the list. Thanks for coming. And thanks for supporting this project. It means a lot to me."

Trey skimmed a hand over her cheek. "I have no doubt you'll make it shine."

Tears sprang to her eyes at his easy confidence. Had he always been this supportive and she just missed it? Maybe all the pressure to perform, to over-achieve, wasn't coming from him at all. God, why was she getting all emotional about this?

Tess wrapped him in a hug. "I love you, Daddy."

"Back atcha, Peanut."

With a modicum of fuss, everybody was finally out the door and on their way back to town. As Mitch shut the front door behind them, Tess dropped into the nearest chair, the weight of the evening crashing down on her. Giddiness warred with exhaustion and the combination left her feeling faintly sick. Because she hadn't just gotten the green light on her passion project and the ability to stay. Grammy had gifted her with a golden opportunity to explore things with Mitch, without the necessity of subterfuge. Tess wanted to jump at the chance to be with him. But it wasn't the same as if he'd invited her into his space himself. He'd looked poleaxed at his grandmother's suggestion.

"So my grandmother is kinda pushy." Mitch sank onto the end of the sofa nearest Tess.

Here it came. He didn't want this. It was too much, too fast. "I couldn't think of a graceful way to do anything but agree with her." Which was true, even if she hadn't *wanted* to disagree at all.

He rubbed his hands along his pant legs, not quite meeting her eyes. "You don't have to move in, Tess. Most of the rest of the family clearly thought it wasn't the best idea, and nobody's going to think any less of you if you choose to stay at the hotel or make other arrangements."

"What about you?" The question spilled out before she could stop it. She was afraid of the answer. Afraid that something had irrevocably changed during dinner and she'd have gained one dream only to have lost another.

"I'd love to have you here." Leaning forward, he reached for her hand. "I *want* you here. Every night. In the mornings. No more sneaking around. But I realize this is fast and a lot and I don't want you to feel pressured—"

"No. No." She stumbled over her words as relief broke over her in waves. "I want to be here."

The carefully neutral expression he'd been wearing since dinner finally cracked. "Yeah?"

Feeling back on solid ground, Tess rose and slid into his lap, looping her arms around his neck. "Of course, I do."

His arms snaked around her waist, feeling like comfort and roots. "The room's yours as long as you want it."

Pausing to choose her words, she skimmed her fingers through his hair. "I'll happily use the office. But I was hoping I'd be sleeping in your bed. I've missed being able to do that since Scotland."

He tightened his embrace. "Thank God. It'll save me the trouble of coming down the hall to sneak into yours."

"So we're settled, then? I'm moving in?"

Mitch grinned. "You're moving in."

Giddiness outweighed the exhaustion. "When?"

"There's no time like the present."

"I like the way you think."

So they drove to The Babylon to pack up her things. It didn't take long. She hadn't planned on being here for longer than a week. As Mitch carried her bags up the stairs, she nudged him toward the guest room.

"Better to be safe than sorry, just in case any members of your large and involved family happened to wander through the house."

"Noted." He shifted directions. "You need more stuff."

"I do. I'll have to call and make arrangements to have some things shipped. I won't be shutting down my flat in London until the project is completely finished, and I'll need to fly back in a month to check on the status of things. I can finish packing things then. But I should be able to have a lot of my clothes and things sent from Denver. And I can pick up some things in the meantime to get me through." She could do with a new capsule wardrobe.

"We can see about a car tomorrow. Meanwhile, how do you feel about a joint bubble bath? You've been tied up in knots for the last few days. We can see what we can do to relieve some of that tension." He ran a finger along her collarbone.

Tess shuddered. "You just keep having the best ideas."

He brushed a soft kiss over her lips. "I'm glad you're here."

"Me too," she sighed.

"I'm gonna go run the bath."

Alone, Tess set to unpacking what little she'd brought, neatly hanging things in the closet, slipping them in drawers. As she organized her toiletries on the bathroom counter, she began to hum. She couldn't remember the last time she'd been this happy and buoyant. Everything was coming up roses.

Her stomach gave a hard, sickening twist. The tube of moisturizer fell from her fingers as she bolted toward the toilet. She barely made it to her knees before she vomited up her dinner.

CHAPTER 8

"*W*ell hey there, sugar. What are you in for today?"

Tess shifted on the exam table, wishing she'd taken the visitor's chair instead as she looked at Piper's cheerful face. "I've been having recurrent nausea. I thought it was food poisoning or a stomach bug, or just a really awful case of jet lag, but it's gone on too long for that. It started on the flight here—I came from London early last week—and every time I think I've shaken it, it comes back. Last night I couldn't even keep down my dinner." A fact she'd been strangely compelled to hide from Mitch. Maybe because once she'd thrown up, she felt fine. Brushed teeth, mouthwash, and back to the plan—which had been well worth not derailing. Still, she'd been nauseous again this morning, so she couldn't keep blaming it on benign causes. Something wasn't right.

Piper went brows up. "When that happened to me it turned out to be Parker."

The mere idea of it made Tess's stomach lurch again. She forced a smile. "Not a possibility." Not with birth control pills and condoms.

Piper waved a hand. "Sorry, it's the curse of new motherhood.

Babies on the brain. Let me take your vitals and get some basic medical history."

Tess nodded, wondering if it had been such a good idea to come to Miranda's clinic about this, especially in the wake of the family's obvious reservations about her moving in with Mitch. God, what would they say if they knew the truth? *Hey Grammy! Thanks for helping me shack up with my vacation fling lover so we don't have to sneak around under everybody's noses!*

She winced.

"I know, that blood pressure cuff is tight, but it'll be done in just a few minutes," Piper assured her.

"It's fine."

"Here, let's check that temperature."

Yeah, in a town the size of Wishful, there weren't that many options. So she'd deal with Miranda. Tess didn't know what to expect of the woman. She'd survived something horrific, and she was, as all the Campbells appeared to be, devoted to the family. Beyond that, Tess was at a loss. She'd been too focused on her presentation, on the dinner, to do more than the very basics of getting to know the other woman.

"Date of last menstrual cycle?"

Tess automatically reached for her planner and flipped back, frowning when she didn't find the relevant notation. But that was just after her trip to Scotland. She'd been off her game, upset about the end of things with Mitch, so she hadn't been as diligent about recording as she normally would.

"Beginning of March. I was doing a lot of traveling, so I can't remember the exact date. But I expect to be starting any day now."

Piper finished making notes in the computer. "All right. You just sit tight. Dr. Campbell will be in to see you shortly."

"Thank you."

As soon as the door closed, Tess put the planner back in her purse and let herself lean back, struggling to get comfortable on the exam table. These things never had any kind of back support.

She must've dozed off because the sound of the door opening had her jerking upright again.

"Well hey there, Tess. I didn't expect to see you this afternoon." Miranda sat down on the stool, setting an iPad on the counter.

Tess expected her to get right to business, but that was not, she was coming to understand, how things were done here.

"So you're moving in with my brother." It wasn't a question, and Tess didn't know what the proper response was, so she said nothing. "Kind of sudden and random, being thrust into a relative stranger's house, even if they are sort of family."

"Mitch doesn't feel like a stranger." At Miranda's arched brow, Tess tried to cover. "I mean, we've spent a fair amount of time together over the past week, working on this proposal, so we've gotten to be friends. He's a good guy. He took me to buy a car this morning so I wouldn't be dependent on him or anybody else."

"He's got a heart of gold," Miranda agreed. "But I want to apologize for him on the front end."

"For what?"

"My brother, God love him, is a compulsive flirt. I don't want you to feel uncomfortable with that."

Tess thought of her own experience on the receiving end of that flirtation and couldn't imagine being uncomfortable with it. He wasn't the skeezy kind of flirt who left a woman feeling like she needed a shower simply by being in the same room. He was charming, dancing his way right past people's reservations, until they wondered why they'd resisted in the first place. By his own admission, he'd dated a huge chunk of the eligible population of women in Wishful. But she'd been all over town with him in the past week, and no one had a cross word or look for him. There was no line of jealous exes or anyone who seemed to expect anything of him—none of the negativity that would follow a player. Because he wasn't one.

Tess felt the urge to defend him. "I'm pretty sure Mitch flirts to put people at ease."

"He does. But a lot of people on the receiving end of that think he's an operator."

"He's a friend. And I'm not uncomfortable." *Please, please leave it at that.*

"Well, all right. I just wanted to check because sometimes Grammy gets something in her head and nobody can make her shake it."

"Your grandmother is adorable." And Tess wanted to kiss her feet for coming up with this arrangement.

"Adorably interfering."

"Interfering with what?"

Miranda shook her head and tapped a few keys on the computer, presumably bringing up Tess's record. "Never mind. So you're having recurring nausea. It comes and goes? Isn't constant?"

"Right."

"Is there a particular time of day it happens?" Miranda put her stethoscope in her ears and pressed it to Tess's chest. "Deep breath."

"Not really. Some days it's lingered for hours. Other times it's just this vaguely queasy feeling that passes."

"Again." She shifted the stethoscope. "What about in relation to eating? Any kind of consistent reaction after consuming food?" She moved the disk around to Tess's back.

"No. Not that I've noticed. I've just felt generally…lousy. I kept chalking it up to other stuff, but it seems unlikely I managed to get food poisoning, jet lag, a stomach bug, *and* anxiety stomach all in the same week."

"I'm inclined to agree with you there. All right. I want to run some basic tests. Do a blood draw, urinalysis, and see what there is to see, okay?"

"Okay."

Tess gave the requisite samples and waited. And waited. It actually probably wasn't more than half an hour, but with nothing to do but stare at the ceiling, it felt longer. At last Miranda stepped through the door, shutting it quietly. Her curiously blank expression set off alarm bells.

"What? What is it? Is it something serious? I mean, I'm twenty-six. I haven't had a proper physical since college other than my annual gynecological exam. I—"

"Calm down. You're perfectly healthy." Miranda sat on the stool and rolled over to the table.

Tess frowned. "Then why am I feeling so sick?"

"You're pregnant."

She opened her mouth but nothing came out. There had to be some mistake.

"I take it this is a surprise?"

Her brain kicked into gear again. "That...that's not possible."

"Unless we're talking you aren't sexually active, immaculate conception kind impossible, I'm afraid it is."

Pregnant? All the blood drained out of her head. Tess dug her fingers into the vinyl of the exam table and fought back a fresh wave of nausea. "But we used protection every time. I'm on birth control!"

"Unfortunately nothing is 100% effective. You said you were traveling a lot. Possibly you didn't take it at the same time every day? There's a three-hour window."

Had she missed that window? Maybe. "But I just had a period a few weeks ago."

"That also happens sometimes. Was it lighter or shorter than usual?"

"I...I thought that was from stress."

"More likely implantation bleeding. Calculating back four weeks earlier, at a guess, I'd say you're seven or eight weeks along."

"I...what? But I wasn't with...anyone until six weeks ago."

"We calculate the due date from the first day of your last period. It tends to be more accurate that way."

"This can't be happening."

"This is clearly a shock."

Shock didn't begin to cover it.

"You'll want to schedule follow up with an OB for a prenatal visit. Taking your birth control in the early weeks of pregnancy isn't usually a risk for miscarriage, but they'll want to confirm everything is as it should be."

"Oh God. Oh God." Tess covered her belly with both hands, as if that would somehow make all this real. Pregnant. With Mitch's baby.

"Hey, hey." Miranda's voice softened. She set the iPad aside and laid a hand on Tess's leg. "I'm sorry. I'm not trying to scare you. There's no reason to think anything is wrong. It's precautionary. Are you and the father in contact?"

Tess whipped her head up, wondering if the truth showed on her face. "I—yes." Jesus. What if she hadn't come here? What if they'd never had this chance second meeting? She'd be dealing with all this alone, not even knowing the last name of her baby's father.

"Okay. You'll need to know his medical history for that first appointment, or as much of it as you can manage. I realize he's in Europe, so that might be difficult. It's not generally the kind of news you want to share over the phone or in an email."

No, he's right here in town. She could tell Miranda right now. But to what end? She didn't know this woman. And it seemed absolutely wrong to tell anyone before Mitch himself.

Miranda hesitated. "Or maybe you would prefer to consider other options?"

Tess lifted her head.

"There is, of course, adoption. And termination."

Termination. Tess flinched at the word. "No." No matter how big a shock, how big a change, how unwelcome this was, terminating this pregnancy would one hundred percent terminate whatever she was building with Mitch. She couldn't do that. Wouldn't.

They spoke a little while longer, with Miranda making some suggestions and offering to give her a referral to an obstetrician in Lawley. Numb, terrified, Tess took the information and got ready to head to the check out. At the last second, she turned back to Miranda. "You can't tell my father."

"Everything we discussed here is protected by doctor-patient confidentiality."

"Okay." Tess blew out a breath. "Okay."

Somehow, she made it out of the office and back into the used Honda she'd picked up that morning. Then she just sat in the parking lot, staring at the planner in her lap as her mind spun. Needing to get back on track, she flipped it open, staring at the details of her life. Nowhere in any of the rigidly lined, carefully written pages did it say *anything* about getting knocked up. So how did this even happen?

Her brain offered up a vivid memory involving her ankles on Mitch's shoulders. Well, okay yeah, she knew how it had happened. But she'd been careful. She'd done all the right things. Except for going way off-book by having an affair in the first place. She opened the pages to the week she'd spent with him in Scotland. Blank but for the sprig of heather she'd pressed between the pages. Because nothing about that week had been planned.

She flipped to her five-year plan. All business and travel. There was nothing on here about having a baby or even finding a guy. There was no room for it in the obsessively detailed list of goals and steps. Was she really going to screw up her entire life, toss out her entire plan, because of that one unplanned week?

And, dear God, what was Mitch going to say? How would he react? It was one thing to cuddle up with your friends' baby. You could give it back to them. It was a whole other thing to have an actual *life* dependent on you.

That was a stupid question. No matter how he really felt about it, he'd ask her to marry him. That was the kind of man he was, how he was made. He'd see that as the right thing to do. And it would utterly destroy everything building between them.

Dropping her head to the steering wheel, she fought back the knot of tears in her throat. She needed to get back to the house. Mitch had client meetings all afternoon. She'd go home, fall apart, and then figure out what to do. Lifting her head, she took another breath, then another as she started the car. But maybe she'd see if Wishful had an office supply store first.

～

"WELL, somebody seems to have gotten his groove back."

Mitch looked up from the construction drawings spread over the hood of his truck and arched a brow at Liam. "Excuse me?"

"I'm just sayin', you don't have that hangdog thing going on anymore. You seem more like your old self. Happy."

Ecstatic was more like, but Mitch had been actively trying to tamp that down the last few days, since he and Tess were keeping things on the down low. No sense inviting questions by giving in to the urge to dance down the sidewalk and click his heels together like the star of some 1950s musical. But he knew he had to give some explanation. "I've got a new project I'm pretty pumped about."

"Yeah? What is it?"

With a soundtrack of nail guns and circular saws behind them, Mitch filled Liam in on the plans to turn the old Heirloom Home Furnishings factory into a small business incubator. "It feels really great to do something positive there to change it, so it doesn't remind Miranda, and doubly good that it's something that will be a boon to the town. I needed to *do* something, and now I am."

"That sounds awesome, man. Is it a Norah project?"

"No, it's Tess's."

"Tess's, huh?"

"Yeah. She'll give Norah a run for her money on top power-house female in town. And if the two team up…God help us all." Mitch couldn't help chuckling at the thought. "I'm pretty sure together they could take over the world."

"That explains it."

He rolled his eyes at Liam's *ah ha* tone. "Dude, cut it with the shit. I'm just happy to be working with good people and doing something useful."

The former Marine didn't look like he bought it, but didn't call Mitch out. "So Tess is sticking around for this whole project?"

"Looks like." Mitch said nothing about their roommate status. By some miracle, it wasn't all over town yet, and he was grateful. At the moment, he wasn't a hundred percent sure how it was going. The last couple of days, Tess had been a little distant and distracted. Was all of this setting up house together too much too soon? Maybe living together had started to take the bloom of excitement off their affair. Or maybe he was just paranoid and her mood had nothing to do with him. Part of this whole cohabitation experiment was getting a sense of real life together. Real life wasn't going to be like the twenty-four-seven, giddy perfection of their vacation fling. And that was fine. The everyday could be just as awesome in its own right.

After finishing up the last of his site visits, Mitch headed home, excited to see Tess. With visions of cracking open a bottle of wine and talking over the day with her as they figured out supper, he stepped into the house, calling out, "Honey, I'm home!" It made him grin. At least until he heard the sound of retching from down the hall.

Ditching the briefcase and drawing tube, he sprinted toward the downstairs powder room. Tess was on her knees over the open toilet, heaving.

"Oh, baby." Mitch stepped inside, automatically scraping her hair back from her face and holding it out of the way as her body betrayed her.

After a couple more minutes, she sank down with a whimper, breathing hard. "Hi." Her voice came out as a croak, like she'd been at this a while.

Mitch tore off some tissue and handed it over. "I was gonna ask how your day went, but I'm guessing not great."

Tess wiped her mouth and leaned against the wall, closing her eyes. "Not so much."

Jesus she was pale. No wonder she'd been acting off. Whatever this was had clearly been building for days and finally just knocked her flat. He wet a hand towel under cold water and wrung it out, laying over her brow.

"Thanks."

"You think that wave is past or do you need to stay in here for a bit?"

"There is literally nothing left in my stomach to throw up."

"Okay then. Up we go." Carefully, he scooped her into his arms.

"You don't have to carry me. I can walk." Her tone was bristly, but her head lolled against his shoulder.

"I expect you can. But you don't have to. What you need is some pjs and good old-fashioned caretaking."

She stiffened. "I can take care of myself."

"Again, not the point. You're sick. Let me take care of you."

"But—"

"No buts. Whatever it is, I've already been exposed, so no reason to quarantine on my account."

She stopped arguing. Mitch carried her upstairs and helped her out of her business attire, into one of his old T-shirts and a pair of her yoga pants. She looked a little better after she'd had the chance to brush her teeth and rinse out her mouth.

"You want to curl up in bed or come downstairs?"

"I'm not a total invalid. Downstairs." She started to go herself, but Mitch just picked her up again.

"I like carrying you."

Tess blew out an irritated breath. He ignored the scowl she shot him as he settled her on the sofa and found a throw. She was an independent woman, used to being in control, so he didn't hold her grumpy patient behavior against her. A stomach bug was about as far from controlled as you could get.

He managed to unearth some crackers and ginger ale. That had always been his mom's go to when he or Miranda had a stomach thing. He poured the ginger ale over ice in one of his sports bottles so she'd have a straw and carried that and the box of crackers back into the living room.

"We'll see how this sits before we try anything more serious. I'm about ninety-five percent sure there's some of Grammy's chicken 'n dumplin's in the freezer. If you can hold this down, I'll heat that up."

Tess accepted the crackers, her eyes lost and a little bit miserable. "I don't—you shouldn't have to do this."

"I don't *have* to do it. I *want* to do it. I don't just want you in bed or for the fun stuff. When I said I wanted a chance at seeing if we can make this work for real, I meant it." And this seemed like damned good practice for the *in sickness and in health* part of that reality. That should probably freak him the hell out.

After a long moment, she clutched the crackers to her chest. "You're really one in a million, aren't you?"

"Mama said God broke the mold the day He made me."

That coaxed a little smile out of her. When he settled on the sofa and she shifted to snuggle up next to him, a bone-deep contentment slid through him. They totally had this real world relationship thing.

Mitch flipped on the TV and navigated over to Netflix to queue up a movie.

"How did you know *Mamma Mia!* is my favorite movie?"

"Because you're too young to have fallen in love with ABBA any other way." As the heroine began to sing the opening number, Mitch started humming along.

Tess cranked her head around to look at him. "You know the music."

"I might have watched it once or twice while I was thinking of you." The mortification of admitting it was worth the total *Aaaaaawww* of her response. "And if you tell my buddies about that, I'll totally lose my man card."

Settling her head against his shoulder, she cuddled in. "Your secret is safe with me."

CHAPTER 9

"*F*eeling better, Peanut?"
Not even a little bit.

But Tess wasn't about to tell her father the reason for that. She'd managed to avoid him for two days on the excuse of a stomach bug, skipping the office and sticking to home. But she couldn't cancel the intimate family dinner with him and Sandy without bringing a horde of well-meaning Campbells armed with soups and casseroles to the house. Right now the house she shared with Mitch felt like a refuge. She didn't think it would stay that way with all of them in it. So here she was, hoping like hell her stomach didn't betray her secret. Even without the morning sickness, she was terrified she had a neon sign hanging over her head. If she got through tonight, it would be a miracle.

How? *How* was she going to tell him about this? How was she going to tell any of them? She didn't even know how to tell Mitch. She'd tried a couple of times the past couple of days and hadn't been able to force the words past her lips. He was so happy with how things were going, just the two of them. She didn't want to destroy that any sooner than she had to.

Tess blinked as she realized Sandy had asked her a question. "Sorry?"

Sandy smiled. "I was just saying we thought you might like a chance to visit without everybody. I tend to forget not everyone's family is a zoo."

"It's a great zoo." Tess was surprised to find she meant it. As overwhelming as the full Campbell clan was, they were all good people. And no matter what happened in the future, they were a part of her life now. They'd be a part of this baby's life.

Her father frowned. "You okay?"

Tess smoothed out her expression, wondering what he'd seen. "Lot on my mind." Which was the absolute truth, but not one she wanted to share.

"Are you sure you're comfortable moving in with Mitch? Because I'm really not. I mean, I know everybody meant well pushing the two of you into that but I really don't think—"

"Dad, I'm twenty-six, not sixteen."

"You're still my baby."

Please don't talk about babies right now. "Mitch is not going to take advantage of me." The taking advantage had been entirely mutual. "Right now, staying at his house suits me. It's practical. I'll stay there until I decide what's next."

Trey crossed his arms. "I don't have to like it."

"No, you don't. But you do have to drop it. What I *meant* was that we have a lot of details to sort out so we're ready to hit the ground running once the purchase of the building is finalized. I need to work out a timeline to completion so I know how long I have to recruit prospective businesses."

His face spasmed a bit as he warred over whether to actually let her change the subject, but eventually he caved. "Norah will have some good ideas about that."

"I'll set up a meeting." She pulled the Hobonichi A6 planner she used for the day-to-day out of her purse and made a note.

They continued discussing the details until Sandy announced

dinner was ready. As soon as they were settled around the kitchen table, Trey clapped his hands together. "I declare business discussion officially closed for the night."

Tess arched a brow and shot him a sideways glance.

"Who are you and what have you done with my daddy?"

He laughed. "I'm still me. I'm just...reprioritizing. I spent a lot of years focused on the company."

That was one way of putting it. He'd retreated from his marriage to her mother through work. Tess had been so conscious of that, she'd begun studying business at ten so as not to lose him any further. What other fifth grader could carry on a cogent discussion of the stock market? Now she didn't know how to talk to him about anything else.

"I don't think Peyton Consolidated would be what it is without that."

He tipped his head in concession of the point. "Maybe not. But it will continue to be what it is without my putting in sixty plus hour work weeks. It will continue to grow without you putting in sixty hour work weeks, too."

The instant wash of panic had Tess setting the bowl of green beans down with a thunk before she dropped it. "Are you unhappy with my performance?"

"Good God no. That would be ridiculous. You've always exceeded my expectations, and I know I've expected a lot. I just don't want you to go down the same path I did and have no life beyond the company. You're twenty-six and, as far as I know, haven't had a serious boyfriend since college."

She stared at him. "Are you seriously sitting there asking me about my love life? Because I'm not discussing that with you." It would come out soon enough, and that was not a conversation she looked forward to.

Color rose in his cheeks. He cleared his throat. "I'm not asking about the details, no. I just wondered if there was anybody serious. I was already married at your age."

"And that worked out so well for you." The words tripped off her tongue before she could think better of it. As soon as they were out, she held up a hand. "I'm sorry, that was uncalled for."

Trey took his time before speaking, glancing over at Sandy, and Tess recognized that he was considering how best to answer. It was a tactic she'd seen him use countless times in boardroom meetings. "Your mother and I had some issues. But they weren't a reflection of our age or the institution of marriage in general."

Yeah, because those issues were all about being forced into marriage because of the oops that had been her. They'd never talked about that with her, but Tess knew. She'd done the math between her parents' anniversary and her own birthday. And during one particularly wine-fueled night after the divorce, her mother had let slip that they'd been on the verge of breaking up when she found out she was pregnant. Knowing that had cast their entire marriage in a whole new light. Given what she'd come from, was it any wonder she wasn't keen on telling Mitch about the baby and ruining everything they were before they'd even really gotten started?

"I'm not in any kind of rush to the altar, Dad. My generation gets around to that later than yours. There's nothing wrong with that." Might as well plant that seed now, because she wasn't about to be browbeaten into marriage because it was the "right thing" to do.

"Of course not. I'm not trying to imply there is. I just...don't want to see you put all of yourself into the company and miss out on anything. I want to see you happy."

"I am happy." Or she had been before her life went completely off the rails. Tess fought back the tide of grief that she wouldn't get to simply enjoy being in love. She didn't have the luxury of regret right now. "I *like* my life. And I love my work." No matter what happened with this baby, she had to be able to hang on to that. Especially since she fully expected the love life portion of the equation to go to hell as soon as she dropped this bomb. "I appreciate that you're having this whole epiphany about work-life balance, and I'm ecstatic that you're happy. I truly am. But I'm good."

And if that wasn't the whole truth, she was a Peyton. She'd work at it until it was.

~

"COME IN! COME IN! HAVE A SEAT." Norah waved to one of the chairs in front of her desk. "Would you like coffee or anything?"

Tess's iffy stomach gave a panicked lurch at the thought. "No, thank you. I'm good." She'd felt almost human as she'd climbed the steps to Norah's City Hall office. She wasn't going to risk changing that.

"How are you feeling?"

Surprise had her dropping the rest of the way into her chair. "Pardon?"

"Oh, Sandy said you'd been sick."

Right. Of course the family would mention something like that. It was normal—expected, even. She had to get her reactions under control.

"I'm feeling okay, thanks." Best get this conversation off that track and onto business. "Dad said you'd be the person to start with to figure out the best means of acquiring candidates for the business incubator."

"I've definitely got some ideas. Cecily will, too, so you'll want to schedule a conversation with her. Do you have some notion of what kind of timeline you're looking at?"

"The purchase of the property should go through by end of next week. I hope to have contractors lined up by then to begin renovations. Like my father, I prefer to use local labor as much as possible, but I expect that will depend on their schedules. Brody is my preference, since he worked for the company for years, but I'm not sure he'll be able to get to it as quickly as I need. Do you have any others to recommend?" She scribbled down names and notes as Norah reeled them off.

"What about capacity? How many businesses do you think you can fit in there?"

"Some of that depends on what kind of businesses they are." Tess went over the refined specs she and Mitch had hammered out.

"I can think of a couple of prospective local businesses that would be a potential fit. But honestly, I'm thinking we'll want to advertise. Candidates will have to apply, right?"

"Yeah. It won't be like somebody just coming in to rent the space. The entire point is for them to accept mentorship, so we'll have to determine if their business concept is a good fit for what we have to offer."

"How will you go about making that determination?"

"Well, the first part of the application process will be the business plan." Tess launched into an explanation of the process and felt some of her anxiety smooth out. This was business. This she knew and understood. At least here she still had some control.

"I haven't finalized the plans, yet but on average, new businesses spend thirty-three months in incubation before moving out on their own. Some programs have formalized benchmarks and graduation. I want to do a bit more research on that front before I present the options to my father, but as our incubator won't be industry specific, I anticipate a pretty diverse selection of businesses."

Norah leaned back in her chair. "I'm impressed with the amount of work you've already gotten done."

Focusing on this project was the only thing keeping her sane right now. Every other waking second, she'd been thinking about the baby, and that whole situation was too overwhelming to focus on for long. But, of course, she couldn't share that.

"This is a passion project of mine, so a lot of the basic groundwork I already had laid out as a concept. I'm just having to adapt it for this location."

"Trey said you were the one who shifted the focus of the company the first time. That you'd talked him into building stuff instead of breaking it up. No more chop shop."

"Dad told you about that?"

Norah smiled. "Yeah. He talks about you all the time."

Tess swallowed against a sudden thickness in her throat. What was that about? She knew her dad loved her. She knew he was proud of her. Why should that make her all emotional? Maybe the pregnancy hormones were already wreaking havoc.

"I took *Pretty Woman* to heart. It just always seemed to me that if you've got the kind of resources Peyton Consolidated has, you have a duty to use them to the betterment of others. Thankfully, he agreed with me. The business incubator is just another way of doing that on a smaller scale. It's that small scale, start-up part of business that's always been my particular interest. It's...personal, I guess. It's not all about boardrooms and billion dollar deals. And there's so much hope and excitement. That's a really good feeling."

"So you think you'll stick around to run it after the center is up and running?"

She'd be having a baby. She couldn't fathom taking that child away from Mitch, and she couldn't imagine taking Mitch away from here. She couldn't keep putting off telling him. They needed to discuss the future and make some decisions together.

"I don't know yet."

Norah smiled. "Well the building process will keep you here long enough to see if small-town life is for you. I'll warn you, though, Wishful has a habit of keeping people who had every intention of going. I was one of them."

"Wishful is charming." And it was. Over the past couple of weeks, she'd spent some time out and about in town, getting the full tour from Mitch and hitting up some of the local watering holes like The Daily Grind and Speakeasy Pizza. The locals had been welcoming, but not in a simpering, suck-up kind of way. And the fact that they didn't make a big deal about the Peyton name or fortune was beyond refreshing. They accepted her because they'd accepted her father. And they'd accepted him because of Sandy. Tess supposed marrying their favorite mayor was a pretty good in.

"Is that the only thing you're finding charming?"

"Excuse me?"

"I'm just wondering how things are going with Mitch. I mean, you were kinda railroaded into it. Are you really okay with this situation?"

"You mean did I say yes just to be polite? No, I didn't."

"Why did you say yes?" There was no suspicion in her tone, just genuine curiosity.

Tess considered her answer. "It seemed...expedient. We're working closely together on this project. And despite my father's enthusiasm for it, I won't know for certain for a few more weeks whether everything will work as I expect. Getting my own place this early seems premature. But taking up the most expensive suite in the hotel is also poor business. Plus, I really am in love with his kitchen." None of that was a lie, even if it wasn't the whole truth.

"It is an amazing kitchen. But is that really all it is?"

"What else would it be?" Tess fought to keep the panic from showing. Did Norah know something? Had they done something to reveal themselves?

"I thought maybe it was because you were uncomfortable around your dad and Sandy."

Tess opened her mouth and closed it again. "Is it that obvious?"

Norah held her thumb and forefinger millimeters apart. "Little bit."

"That was not my intention. Sandy is a really lovely woman. I just...don't have any idea how to behave around her. I don't really have any idea how to behave around your entire family. I am an only child of divorced parents."

"Me too."

"Really?"

"Yeah. I come from prime, Type A, overachiever stock. And I thought for a long time that meant I couldn't have my career and a solid relationship. The Campbells helped teach me I was wrong."

"I can see how that would be the case. It seems like everybody in the family is paired off in some ideal relationship." It still felt a little unnatural to Tess.

"They're great people. Often nosy, interfering, and over-whelming, but always well-intentioned. And yeah, other than Ava —she's Reed's sister. She's a photojournalist working in Afghanistan right now—and Mitch, everybody's paired off."

"You've known him a long time? Mitch, I mean."

"We've been friends almost as long as Miranda and I have. I met him when she brought me home with her from college, and he's always been like my very flirty older brother. But flirtation aside, he's as loyal as they come. And honorable. So don't have any concerns that he might take advantage of you."

"That hadn't even crossed my mind." How could it? The idea was laughable. The man had ignored her less than graceful accep-tance of his help and taken care of her. He'd fed her chicken and dumplings and watched her favorite movie. And he'd been content to simply hold her. If anything, it had felt like she was taking advantage of him. Especially with this secret hanging over her head. But she'd fix that. And she'd just have to hope and pray that the news wouldn't be the death knell she believed it to be.

CHAPTER 10

The house was too quiet when Mitch got home. Tess's car was in the garage, so unless she'd gone off with somebody else, she had to be here. Maybe she was napping. She'd been awfully tired since that stomach flu. Not that she'd appreciated it when he suggested she was working too hard and ought to take it easy. Tonight he'd opted for sneakier tactics to achieve the same end. He was cooking dinner. It wouldn't be on par with the Italian feast she'd made or even the everyday gourmet fare she tended toward, but by damn, he could grill. After stowing the groceries he'd picked up on the way home, he went to search her out.

Moving into the dark living room, he switched on a light, pulling up short when he spotted her curled in a chair, a mug in her hands. "Hey." He knew before the word even fell from his lips that something was very wrong. Her expression was too set, too serious.

"Hi." She didn't smile.

Mitch searched her face. Had she been crying? "Baby, what's wrong? Is there a snag with the project? Did you have a fight with your dad? Has somebody died?"

She shook her head. "Would you please sit down?" The fingers around her mug were white.

Dread curled through his gut as he moved toward her. "Why do I feel like I should do that with a glass of bourbon?"

"You may want some before this is over."

That didn't bode well. But he sat without it, taking the end of the sofa nearest her and hating that he couldn't easily touch her and try to comfort. Or maybe he wanted some comfort for himself.

Tess took a measured breath, staring into the mug. "I've been trying to think how to tell you this for days."

She's breaking up with me. The sick certainty of it hit him like a sucker punch. He couldn't imagine any other reason she'd look so grave and uncomfortable. Their days together, both here and in Scotland, spun through his head in a jumbled loop. His mind tried to sift through, to find a reason, to suss out some argument he could use to combat what was coming. But all he saw were the best days of his life. If she didn't feel the same, how could he change her mind?

She lifted her gaze to his, steeling herself. "There's no good way to ease into this, so I'm just going to rip the Band-aid off."

Their living together was too much, too soon. That had to be it. She'd decided she couldn't handle this. Mitch braced himself for the blow, wondering if the knowing it was coming would lessen the inevitable pain or make it worse.

"I'm pregnant."

Her words stopped the montage flying through his brain on fast forward. "What?"

"I haven't had the stomach flu or jet lag or food poisoning. I am, impossibly, improbably, pregnant."

They weren't breaking up. Relief came hard and fast, forcing his breath out on a wheeze. If he hadn't already been sitting, his legs would've gone right out from under him. His worst fear hadn't come to pass. But what she'd said.... Mitch struggled to kick his brain in gear. Holy shit. A baby. They'd made a baby. How had that even happened? They'd taken steps, used protection.

What did it matter? Tess was pregnant with his child.

This was the why of everything. Why she'd been sick. Why she'd been distant.

It was his wish come true. Maybe not at all what he'd imagined when he made it, but a baby meant marriage and family and everything he wanted, everything he hadn't gotten a chance to ask for in Scotland because their time had been over too soon. Now they'd get their forever.

"Please say something." It was as close to pleading as he'd ever heard from her, and he realized she still sat there, white-knuckling her mug, utterly terrified of his reaction.

He surged to his feet, not missing her flinch as he plucked the mug from her hands.

Her face fell. "I'm sorry."

"Sorry? Honey—" Mitch grasped her hands, tugging her up from the chair and into his arms. "I'm gonna be a daddy! This is amazing!" He spun them in circles before it occurred to him that might upset her stomach.

Tess's mouth pulled into a frown. "You're...happy?"

"I'm thrilled! I mean, okay, it's a shock. But a baby. My mom will be over the moon. The first Campbell grandbaby. *Everybody* will be over the moon. We'll have to dive into planning the wedding. And a nursery! That room a couple doors down from ours would be ideal, I think. Good space. Room for a kid to grow. I've got lots of ideas. I think I went through about a dozen designs for Autumn and Judd..."

He trailed off as he realized Tess hadn't responded to any of his ramble.

She stared up at him, expression guarded. "You're making a helluva lot of assumptions."

Mitch replayed everything he'd just spouted off, not seeing the problem. "I'm just being logical. We're having a baby. Of course we're getting married."

"No. We're not."

As he looked at her—really looked at her—he realized she wasn't anywhere near as excited about this as he was. He didn't see any of the bubbling joy. He saw...resignation.

"You're not happy about this."

"Of course I'm not happy!" She tugged away from him and reached for a book on the table, waving it at him. "Nowhere in my planner does it say 'Have affair. Get pregnant. Destroy plan.'" Clutching the planner to her chest, she sank down onto the couch. "I've been freaking out for days. I didn't plan on this. In fact, I planned very specifically to avoid this."

He sat beside her and laid a hand on her knee, needing the connection. "For right now or forever?" It hadn't even occurred to him she might not want children. But she hadn't exactly been for the idea when the topic came up at the diner with Cam and Norah, had she?

"It hardly matters, does it? Like it or not, my entire life is going to change." The words were bitter, her tone full of frustration. "And this isn't like a little change to the plan, where I can hide the mistake with washi tape and stickers. This is a have to start from fucking scratch with a new plan kind of change."

"What the hell is washi tape?" Seeing the narrowing of her eyes, he realized now was absolutely not the moment for that question. "Never mind."

She hadn't chosen this. Neither had he. But at thirty-four, he was a lot more settled in his life, in his career. This wasn't a blessing or the answer to a wish for her. It was an atomic bomb to her carefully laid plans. So maybe rushing ahead to the happily ever after was premature and telling her they were getting married instead of actually asking had been a mistake. He'd table that for now and rectify it later.

"When are we going to tell everyone?"

The color drained out of her cheeks. "We're not telling anybody. Not yet. I'm only seven or eight weeks along. I could still miscarry. I'm sure as hell not dropping this bomb on our families until I know for sure it's going to stick."

That was fair. There'd be a lot of explaining to everybody that he wasn't exactly looking forward to. But miscarriage. Jesus. Just the word sent a bolt of fear straight through him. He wanted to scoop her up and wrap her in cotton to protect her and what she carried from the world. That was his son or daughter inside her.

"Have you been to the doctor yet?"

"Miranda."

"My sister knows?"

"Not about you. I went to see her on Monday to figure out why the hell I've been so sick. I haven't been to an OB yet. My appointment is in Lawley tomorrow."

"What time do we leave?" He'd cancel or reschedule whatever he had to.

"We?"

Mitch leaned in to cup her face, running a thumb along the arch of her cheek. "I'm in for this, Tess. One hundred percent. You're not alone."

After a long moment, she slid her arms around him, resting her cheek against his shoulder, but he could tell she didn't quite believe him. He didn't know yet how to make this easier on her. For now, he'd simply be there, every step of the way.

"You can keep your top on, but remove everything on the bottom and take this drape and have a seat on the exam table. Dr. Jenkins will be with you shortly."

"I'll just be over here." Mitch sank into the visitor's chair.

As soon as the door to the exam room shut, Tess scooped up the drape and slipped behind the curtain to change. She was acutely aware of Mitch on the other side. She couldn't decide if it was better or worse to have him here. It was one thing to talk abstractly about the possibility of miscarriage. But somewhere in the midst of the eleven thousand questions about her medical history and his, she'd started to worry about what they'd find out on this visit. Whether this pregnancy was viable or not, it changed things between her and Mitch. There was no going back to the way things were before, and that scared her to death, making her wish she'd confirmed things for sure before bringing it up and bought them a little more time to be...just them.

Feeling self-conscious, Tess clutched the edges of the drape together like a wrap skirt and circled around to sit. The crinkle of paper and creak of vinyl was too loud in the exam room. Rearranging the drape across her lap, she was acutely aware of her bare butt against the paper. Really, nobody should have to face life-changing news without pants. She didn't know what to say. Small talk hardly seemed appropriate right now. So she stewed in silence, thinking of her mother.

What had she felt in this moment? Was she scared? Angry? Had she been excited, despite the less than auspicious circumstances of her pregnancy? Tess realized she didn't even know if her dad had been at that appointment, if he'd even known about her yet. She definitely hadn't been planned. They'd already been on the verge of breaking up. And then Tess had come along and they'd gotten married instead because Mom came from a good Catholic family and her dad had an iron-clad sense of duty. And now here she was, twenty-six years later, as history repeated itself. Like mother like daughter.

Her chest went tight.

The scrape of the chair had her looking up. Mitch dragged it beside the exam table and sat again, reaching over to fold the hands she'd been wringing in his.

"Look at me."

She lifted her head to meet his clear, steady gaze.

"Everything is going to be fine." His tone held conviction and maybe a promise.

Tess wanted to relax, wanted to trust him. But she couldn't let go of the fear. *What if it's not?*

The door opened and the doctor came in. A petite African American woman, with short, natural hair, shot through with gray, and fathomless dark eyes behind wire-rimmed glasses, Gloria Jenkins radiated calm. Tess felt like maybe she'd seen everything in her thirty years of practice and would know what to do. She really wanted somebody who knew better to tell her what to do.

They made introductions all around.

"This is your first child?"

Tess found she couldn't actually speak, so she just nodded.

"Okay. The initial tests look good. I'll get through the physical exam as quickly as possible, and then we'll do an ultrasound to verify how far along you are."

"Do you want me to step out?" Mitch asked.

Did she? This was a weirdly intimate thing. And yet there was no part of her body he hadn't seen before. If he let go of her hand, she might start freaking out again. Tess shook her head, and he squeezed her fingers.

She scooted to the end of the exam table and stared up at the ceiling. It wasn't much different from her annual gynecological check-up, except for the fact that Mitch was here. He watched her face, not what was going on down by the stirrups. Ever the gentleman.

"We should start talking about names," he said.

"Names?"

"Sure. I'm partial to Delbert Bodine for a boy and Orpha Louise for a girl."

Tess stared at him in horror. "If you're serious, Mitch Campbell, I'm walking away from you right now, pants be damned. You can't be trusted."

He cracked a grin, the corners of his eyes crinkling. That smile did something to her, unraveling some of the knots of tension.

"You're evil. You know that, right?"

"Gotcha thinking about something else, didn't it?"

For all of twenty seconds anyway. "Sneaky man."

Dr. Jenkins rolled over the ultrasound machine. "With the date of your last period, you should be right at eight weeks along, so we're going to confirm that."

Tess moved to lift up her shirt.

"Oh, no honey. This early the baby's too small to see on an external sonogram. It's about the size of a raspberry right now. We'll be using this transducer to do an internal one." She held up a sort of wand that looked for all the world like a dildo. The condom on it didn't help that impression.

"Um." Tess didn't know what to say.

Mitch made a small choking noise, as if holding back a laugh.

Dr. Jenkins chuckled. "Yeah we get that reaction a lot. Lie on back now. You'll feel a little pressure."

Tess jerked, everything in her going tense again at the alien sensation.

"Just try to relax now."

She took a few deep breaths, aware she was clenching Mitch's hand like a vise.

He pressed a kiss to the back of her hand. "You're doing great."

God how could he be so *calm*? Did he not realize the enormity of all of this?

Shapes appeared on the monitor. Dr. Jenkins made a few adjustments.

"Ah, here we go."

And there it was, in stark black and white. A distinct baby-shaped thing. With feet! And an actual face. Or the profile of one, at least. Something was moving. A rapid little flutter that said, *Hey, I'm alive.*

"Mitch." Tess could barely do more than whisper his name, but he squeezed her hand tight.

"Ho-ly shit," he murmured.

Dr. Jenkins pointed to the fluttery bit. "That right there is the heartbeat. Good and strong."

"It's so fast," Tess said. "Why is it so fast? Is something wrong?"

"Fast is totally normal. You have a healthy baby here."

"Healthy baby. Okay. Okay." The relief flooding through her was staggering. Healthy baby. With everything else going on and all the terror over the changes, she hadn't even realized how worried she'd been about that. There was a part of her—a small, selfish part, that had wanted this situation to take care of itself. To just wake up and have it over. A bad dream.

But this wasn't a problem. It wasn't a mistake. It was a *child*. Her child. And maybe she was taking a little while to get on board with that, but she was in it now. They had a healthy baby and they were doing this thing.

She just had to figure out if they could actually do it together.

itch stared at the ultrasound as Dr. Jenkins pointed out various features and talked about different signs of the baby's stage of development. That was a real, live baby in there. His baby. That little lima bean was his son or daughter. It kinda looked like a big-headed alien at the moment, but it was distinctly headed toward human-shaped. A freaking miracle.

He and Tess had done that. They'd made that, despite all the odds. It had to mean something, didn't it? Like the hand of Fate ensuring they'd be together. How could they not? All the stars were aligning.

Mitch wanted to hug Tess. To kiss her. In truth, he wanted to make love to her all over again. But when he shifted his attention to her, wanting to share the bubbling joy, she didn't look at him. He couldn't read the expression on her face as she continued to stare at the screen. She wasn't saying a word. She'd loosened the stranglehold on his fingers after Dr. Jenkins declared the baby healthy, but he couldn't tell if she was really tuned in to what was being said or not. So he was the one who finally released her hand to take notes and ask a thousand questions. He made lists of things to research, topics he and Tess needed to discuss and decide. The recommended reading alone was staggering. It would be the most he'd studied since he got out of grad school. And all the options for genetic testing... Dear Lord. They had seven months to do what felt like seven years' worth of planning.

"Do you have any more questions?"

Mitch shot Tess a look, but she was still staring at the now blank screen. "I'm sure we'll think of many, many more, but for now, I'd say we're at information overload."

"It's a lot to process. Make yourself a list and bring it back when I see you in four weeks. If you have any problems, you can always call my nurse. She'll get me if it's anything worrisome. But all I see are signs of a healthy pregnancy, so I don't expect you'll need to."

"Thank you, Dr. Jenkins."

If she thought it was weird that he'd done almost all the talking, she didn't let on. Tess roused herself enough to thank the doctor when she handed over the sonogram. Then they were alone. Tess slid off the table and went behind the curtain to dress.

Not knowing what else to do, he started talking. "That was... amazing. Mind-bogglingly awesome."

Nothing.

"I know you'll want to keep this on the down low for a while longer, so I figured we'd run by a pharmacy here to pick up your prenatal vitamins. And we might as well hit up a bookstore to grab some of these books the doc suggested. It's a minor family sin to buy books anywhere but at Inglenook, but under the circumstances, I think we can make an exception."

Still, Tess said nothing. Unease began to creep in. Why wasn't she talking?

The curtain slid back. Tess's gaze was fixed on the sonogram picture in her hands. When she lifted her face to his, her big brown eyes glimmered with a sheen of tears. Even as she took a step forward, the first one slid down her cheek.

"We're having a baby." The words were a raw whisper.

Mitch's gut clenched. Not tears. Anything but tears. He didn't know how to fix this for her. Didn't have a clue how to suppress his own happiness at the very thing she thought ruined her life.

Then she smiled, and it was like a sunrise lighting up her face. All the dark and dread and anxiety that had been haunting her for days faded. And Mitch realized that it hadn't been upset keeping her quiet. It simply hadn't been real for her yet. Not until this moment.

"We're having a baby." Grinning, he gave in to the jubilation and scooped her into a twirling hug. She was laughing as he set her on her feet, and he was struck, hard and fast, as he had been that night he'd seen her on the little pub stage. She was so beautiful, so perfect, and now, so his.

I love you.

The words hovered at the tip of his tongue. But he stayed them, as he'd stayed them countless times since she'd walked back into his life. He'd told himself it was too much, too soon. She'd bolted from what was between them before. He hadn't wanted to scare her. But if he told her now, would she think it was only because of the baby? Would she understand that he'd loved her all along? Would she believe him? He didn't know, and until he did, declarations had to wait.

Wanting to keep that smile on her face, he laced his hands at the small of her back. "How about we go get those vitamins, pick up the books, and then maybe think about checking out furniture for Topenga Marie's nursery."

"Topenga Marie?"

"Or Cletus Clyde. I'm flexible."

"What you are is incorrigible." But she was still smiling as she leaned in to kiss him. "I was thinking more like Balvenie. Because

I'm reasonably sure that distillery tour may be why this baby exists."

He considered. "You know, that's not actually half bad. We could do the whole nursery in plaid."

"With fuzzy sheep and Highland coos." She giggled at her own terrible Scots accent.

"And a night light made out of a whiskey bottle?"

"That might be taking the theme too far."

"We can negotiate." He could think of a whole host of fun ways to settle terms.

"For now, let's get the vitamins and the books and go home. I want some time to sit with this whole thing and get used to the idea." She pressed a kiss to his cheek and rose to her toes, so her breath tickled his ear. "And I'd really like to reenact that afternoon after the distillery tour."

Already hard, Mitch turned toward the door. "Check please!"

"You got me baby-themed washi tape." Tess had to force the words past the lump in her throat.

"I did. And since we don't know if it's a boy or a girl, I went with both. Do you know how expensive that shit is? I can buy you like eight rolls of 2", high-quality painter's tape for the cost of one of those little bitty things!"

Tess clutched both tubes of decorative tape to her chest and thought her heart might just explode for love of this man. She had no idea how he'd managed to sneak that by her when they picked up all the books. "Thank you."

He drew her in, wrapping his arms around her. "I know how hard all this is for you. I know this isn't much, but I just wanted to do something to make you smile."

It was tape. It didn't fix anything, didn't make the situation any less stressful. But he'd remembered and he'd thought of her. And that, more than anything he'd said since he found out, made her feel less alone.

"Mission accomplished. Let's go home."

The whole drive, Tess listened to Mitch throw out more awful names as he talked about plans for the nursery and a life of little league and dance recitals, Christmas mornings and family traditions. He was legit, no faking, ecstatic about this baby. She still couldn't quite wrap her brain around that. But neither could she stop herself from getting kind of excited herself about this Norman Rockwell life he was painting. He didn't bring up marriage again, and that was a relief. Right now he was focused on the baby and the future. And that future included her at every turn. Tess was too practical to believe it would unfold exactly as he envisioned. But maybe...maybe, she and Mitch stood a chance where her parents hadn't. They certainly hadn't started out with this much joy at the prospect of family. Letting herself believe that, having some hope—dangerous though it was—lifted an enormous weight off her heart.

She'd thought he'd forgotten her request for that reenactment, but they'd barely made it inside before he backed her against a wall and took her mouth, his hands already beneath the hem of her shirt, tugging it up. He broke the kiss to strip it off, and she yanked at his shirt to do the same. They bumped through the kitchen, kissing, touching, taking, leaving a trail of clothes in their wake. When Mitch would have driven them up the stairs, she dragged him into the living room. The sofa was closer, and after all, once the baby came, it would be harder to give in like this wherever, whenever they felt like it.

Naked, they tumbled onto the couch, and nothing had ever felt as good as the weight of all his warm skin against hers. His hands were everywhere, stroking her to a fever pitch. God, she loved his hands, loved the hard body beneath hers, loved what he could do to her. Needing him inside her, she moved to straddle his hips, until his cock nudged her entrance.

"Wait," he croaked. One hand flailed toward the floor, where they'd left his pants. Condom.

Tess, cupped his cheek. "I think that's a little like shutting the barn door after the horses are already out."

He paused. "Sure?"

"I need you. Just you." She kept her eyes on his as she sank down, slowly taking him in. She watched emotion and pleasure bloom in his eyes as he murmured her name and knew this wouldn't be the fast, frantic coupling she'd imagined.

He drew her down for a kiss, seducing her with his mouth as she began a slow, steady rhythm. So much of their lovemaking had been flash and fire, always with that edge of desperation because their time had been finite. But this...there was patience here and a trust that there was time. There was a future. Together. Years to learn and grow and love. So she gave herself over to the dream, to him. Patience mated with passion, driving them both higher, longer, until she cried out from the joy of it and he emptied inside her.

Slumping boneless and sated on his chest, her heart was full to bursting. *I love you. I love you. I love you.* The words wanted to spill out like the music of a full gospel choir. But she held herself back, not wanting to hear a reflexive response that was really just about the baby. Instead, she set out to lighten the mood.

"I wonder if on-purpose conceptual sex is that amazing."

Mitch stroked a possessive hand over her ass. "I don't know, but I vote we find out."

She propped up enough to give him the side eye. "That ship has sailed. Or was it so good that you forgot where we spent the afternoon?"

His grin made her heart pinch. "For right now I know, but I never imagined having just one kid. I mean, Ephegenia Doreen needs a brother or sister. What about you?"

Were they really having this conversation? Well, if not now, then when? If they were building a life together, the question of how many kids was relevant. "I hadn't ever given it much thought. I'm an only child, so that seems normal to me. But I can see how multiples would be normal for you. Let's see how we do with Bertis Lamont before we go all Cheaper By The Dozen or whatever."

He snickered. "We're gonna do great."

"I'm glad one of us is confident."

He rolled, toppling her from her perch to tuck her against his side and lay a hand on the slope of her belly. "I can't wait to see you get all round."

Wincing at the image and not at all enthused about the idea of a preggo body—the women in her family tended to pack it on during pregnancy—she just looked at him. "Seriously? You're looking forward to me turning into a waddling cow?"

"First off, there is no possible circumstance under which I won't find you sexy. Second, there's something really primal about seeing your woman pregnant. I mean maybe it's all caveman biological imperative or whatever, but it's sexy as hell."

She should *not* find that caveman attitude appealing. But she did. Maybe it was that casual, possessive way he'd called her his woman. She wanted to be his woman. She wanted to be his everything. "Hang on to that thought for when my ankles are the size of an elephant's."

"I'll have you know, I give killer foot massages. And back rubs. I'm going to take care of you, Tess." Sincerity shone in his eyes.

Her throat went thick. "I'm not great at being taken care of. But for you, I'll work on it."

Mitch brushed a soft, reverent kiss over her lips, making her hum. As he stroked a hand down her leg, she felt the stirrings of fresh arousal. "You know, those ankles aren't the size of an elephant's now."

She slanted him a look. "No, they are not. Why?"

"Because I'm thinking you could probably get them over my

shoulders." At her arched brow, he grinned. "You did say you wanted a reenactment."

"I did say that." She gave a long, luxurious stretch, loving the way his hungry gaze drank in her body. "Well, in the name of taking advantage as long as I can…"

CHAPTER 12

"Well, look who decided to show up." From his chair at the poker table set up on his screened in porch, Judd jerked a thumb toward the house. "There's beer and pizza."

Mitch saluted him and the rest of the gathered players before heading inside. He deposited his own six-pack in the fridge and grabbed one of the cold long-necks before loading up a paper plate with pizza from Speakeasy and carrying it back outside. He took the chair between Liam and Reuben Blanchard, who wore the dealer's hat.

"The prodigal son returns!" Liam crowed. "We were beginning to think you'd abandoned us."

Mitch so wasn't about to address the fact that he hadn't actually been to poker night since before his trip to Europe, so he'd take the ribbing as his due. "Yeah, yeah. It's good to see y'all, too." He twisted off the top and took a pull on his beer. "Cam's got a City Council meeting. Ethan coming?"

"On babysitting duty," Darius Greeley announced. "We picked up a speeder with a rap sheet the length of my arm. County's coming to pick him up, but they couldn't get here until tomorrow, so somebody had to stick around the station. Ethan drew the short straw."

"Looks like it's just us tonight, then. Let's get this party started." Reuben began to shuffle. "Where you been, Campbell?"

"Busy." Understatement of the century.

The ex-SEAL cut Mitch a glance. "That got something to do with your pretty new roommate?" He said roommate in a tone of air quotes.

Irritation prickled, but Mitch knew he couldn't rise to the bait. "That setup was Grammy's idea. You know nobody says no to her."

Judd picked up the cards he'd been dealt and studied them. "Seems to be working out. You've been spending an awful lot of time at home."

He'd have been there tonight if not for the fact that Norah had sweet-talked Tess into teaching her how to make the agnolotti. But this was good. He needed to reconnect with his pals and get at least a few things back to the status quo.

"We're working on a project for her dad. Repurposing the old Heirloom Home Furnishings factory." Mitch relaxed a bit as he told them about the project and studied the flop against his own hand. He discarded two cards and took two more. "Plus, I've been catching up on everything that got put on hold during my vacation."

"Speaking of, you finally gonna tell us about that trip?" Liam asked.

Reuben added the turn. "Yeah, you were gone almost a month. Where all did you go?"

Mitch didn't see the harm in talking about it now. "It was a blast. Rhett and I were in Paris for the conference for a week. Then we worked our way through Italy, Germany, Switzerland, and Austria before heading over to the UK."

"Oh, how was that? My wife is pushing me for a British vacation next summer. She's obsessed with *The Great British Bake Off* and wants to do some kind of food tour of the region." Darius changed out three of his cards. "Raise."

Mitch met the bet and tossed in a couple more chips. "It was good. We toured London extensively, the Lake District, Cambridge. Headed down to Wales, and up into Scotland."

"Yeah? Did you make it up to the Highlands?" Judd raised the bet again.

Reuben turned over the river.

"Yeah. It's gorgeous." Mitch studied his hand. Queen high flush. He could work with that. He adjusted his final bet and added some more chips to the pot. "Bunch of distilleries to tour. Loch Ness and all that."

"Any sightings of Nessie?" Liam teased.

"No, but lots of old castles. The fact that so many of them have survived is amazing. Some have been restored to fully functioning estates for the tourists, so you can see how they used to live way back when. And there are plenty of dudes in kilts to make the ladies happy."

Liam grimaced. "I don't want to encourage that. Riley might make me wear one."

Judd leaned back in his chair, eyes narrowed in consideration. "I don't know. Seems like there might be something to be said for easy access."

"You are not wrong. I tried one on while I was there, just for the hell of it. It was surprisingly comfortable."

Everybody laid down their cards. Mitch scanned the hands. Looked like Darius was raking in the pot. Damn him.

"Tess couldn't talk you into buying it?" Judd asked.

Mitch snorted, remembering that whole negotiation. "Oh, she tried, but—" He cut himself off with a curse.

Judd dropped his chair back to all four legs and pointed at Liam. "Called it. Pay up."

Liam tossed a twenty across the table. "So you knew her before she got here."

"That's low man. Pulling out interrogation tactics during poker." Mitch scowled. "How did you know?"

"Deduction, my dear Campbell. Autumn was admiring Tess's necklace at the cookout, and Tess mentioned how it was a gift from a recent trip to Scotland. Add to that the fact that since you got home, you've looked like you lost your best friend. Yet as soon as she got to town, you lit up like the Fourth of July. Neither of you could stop looking at each other that night. Seriously, don't either of you commit a crime. You can't lie worth a damn. You and Tess Peyton are not just roommates."

It seemed pointless to deny. "Who else knows?"

Judd went brows up. "Far as I know, just the people at this table."

"Keep it that way. We don't want the family to know yet."

"Why is it a big deal for y'all to be involved?" Reuben asked, dealing the next hand. "You're both single, consenting adults."

"It's complicated." And while it felt good for *someone* to finally know about them, he wasn't about to be revealing Tess's pregnancy to his poker buddies before they told anybody else.

"Is it complicated because it's a fling with a woman connected to your family or is it complicated because it's serious?" Liam asked.

Darius laughed. "Since when does Mitch ever do serious?"

Mitch tugged his wallet out of his back pocket and fished out the proof of his intention to lay on the table. "Since now."

The four of them stared at the diamond ring glittering against the green felt.

"Well, holy shit," Judd murmured. "I didn't call *that.*"

"How long have you known this woman?" Reuben asked.

"Long enough."

Judd studied him with those detective's eyes that saw too much. "You sure about this?"

"As sure as I've ever been of anything in my life."

He nodded. "Well all right then. Congratulations."

"Hang on to that. She hasn't said yes yet. I'm still trying to work my way around to the best way of asking her." He'd flubbed it after she'd told him about the baby, so he knew it was essential he get this right.

"Let me get this straight." Liam abandoned his cards to lean on the table. "You two aren't telling your family that you're involved and plan to just spring it on them with a 'Hey, we're engaged!'?"

To Mitch's mind, that seemed way better than leading off with, "Hey, we're pregnant!"

"I've got a reputation with women. Nobody seems to be able to grasp the idea that I could actually be serious about one, and I'd just as soon start off with that fact crystal clear. So, yeah, right now, that's the plan."

"Okay then," Reuben said, turning the river. "Let's talk proposal strategy."

～

"HEY! COME ON INSIDE." Norah opened the door with a sweeping, warm welcome.

Tess couldn't quite figure out how she'd ended up here tonight, except that when Norah had asked her for a lesson in how to make agnolotti, she couldn't think of a reason to say no. And, in truth, aside from Mitch, she'd felt pretty isolated since she got to Wishful. She missed having girlfriends. Not that she was at all sure if she could *be* girlfriends with Norah, but that was definitely her issue. Her father's golden girl had been nothing but open and friendly since she arrived.

In the kitchen, she set down the bag of supplies she'd brought and noticed a deep blue leather planner on the counter. "Is that the Chic Sparrow Pemberley?"

Norah's eyes took on the familiar gleam of a fellow planner addict. "It is! I just got it this year. I needed something new after planning the wedding and thought I'd try a traveler's notebook. Are you a Chic Sparrow fan?"

"I've been lusting after the new Outlander collection. I just love the leather, but I haven't been able to settle on what size I want."

They fell into animated discussion of size options and features as Tess unloaded and spread out ingredients, walking Norah through the making of the pasta dough. She found she really *liked* this woman. Who else had she met recently who had the same favorite Etsy suppliers for custom planner accessories? Norah got it. And that just felt a little weird given her relationship with Tess's dad.

Wrapping the dough in plastic wrap, Tess popped it into the fridge. "This needs to chill at least thirty minutes, so we'll get started on the filling. You can stuff it with all kinds of things. My favorite is actually portabella mushrooms with ricotta and herbs, but the chicken and spinach is Dad's favorite, so that's what I went with for dinner and for tonight. We're going to need a six-quart pot and a skillet."

Norah pulled the requested pieces out. "You know, I'm really envious of your relationship with your dad."

Tess stared at her. "You're jealous of *me?*"

"Yeah. Little bit. My dad's nothing like yours. Trey is great at recognizing that everybody's got their own interests and strengths and playing to that. My dad..." She shook her head. "I was raised with all this pressure that Burkes are meant to do great things. You get that. You've got a big family legacy, too."

Tess inclined her head in acknowledgment.

"I absolutely took that edict to heart. But my dad's expectations and the expectations I believed he had for me weren't the same thing."

"What do you mean?"

"Dad had it in his head that I was going to follow in his footsteps and go to law school. The only acceptable deviation would have been med school to take after my mother. I did something entirely different that he's never approved of. So I've spent my entire adult life trying to meet his expectations and failing."

"Then his expectations are bullshit. Look at what you've done here. You have absolutely proved yourself. You saved an entire freaking town."

"With a small army."

"Maybe so but my dad never talks about the army. Just you. Frankly, it feels like a lot to live up to."

Now Norah was the one staring. "Tess, do you think Trey's *comparing* us?"

The tone of absolute shock had Tess wishing she'd kept her mouth shut. She shrugged and braced herself, accepting that they were finally going to address the elephant in the room. "You cast a wide shadow, Wonder Woman."

Norah pressed her hands to the counter and seemed to work on gathering her thoughts. "Do you have any idea how much your dad talks about you? About how proud he is of all the things you've done? All the things you want to do? Do you have any idea what I'd give for my dad to just *once* acknowledge that I'm good at what I do and that he's proud of me? Sure, Trey is impressed with what I've done, and I appreciate the hell out of that. But it's not the same. There's a part of me that's still trying to live up to the family name. You've already lived up to yours."

Tess rocked back on her heels and absorbed that. She'd already lived up to the family name? If that were true, then exactly who was she trying to impress with all the backbreaking work? As she stood across from this woman she'd seen as a rival, she found she didn't have an answer. She scooped a hand through her hair. "So I'm jealous of you, you're jealous of me, and we're both probably being ridiculous?"

"It does rather look that way."

Tess couldn't help but laugh at the absurdity of it. "Jesus. We really are a lot alike."

Norah grinned. "People do keep saying that. The fact is, Tess, we have a lot in common, and I'd really like to be friends."

Tess really, really wanted a friend. "I'd like that. Now give me that skillet." Norah handed it over, and Tess added a pat of butter, setting it to melt. "So where is Cam tonight?"

"He had a City Council meeting. Where's Mitch?"

"Poker night. I believe there was some discussion of handcuffs and hog-tying if he didn't show up this week. Here, go ahead and clean off these mushrooms and give them a rough chop."

Norah peeled the plastic wrap off the package and began wiping down the mushrooms with a damp towel. "Judd and Liam take poker night very seriously. Cam only gets a pass because he's got official city business."

Tess found herself curious about these guys Mitch was closest to. "They've been friends for a long time?"

"Since grade school. They're good guys."

"Judd is the detective, right? Married to Autumn? The pregnant one."

"Yeah, that's them. There's a love story for the ages." Norah began chopping the mushrooms. "Those two were best friends from the time they were six. It took forever for them to get out of their own way and admit they were in love with each other, but once they got past that hurdle, they didn't waste any time. Judd proposed and presented Autumn with a fully planned wedding on the same day."

"Seriously?" Tess added the diced onion to the skillet.

"Seriously. As long as it took Cam and me to even set a date, I'll admit to some jealousy there. I think Riley's got some of that going on, too. She and Liam have been trying to plan their wedding around his brothers' deployments."

She added the ground chicken to the pan with the onions. "What's their story?"

"Oh, that was fun to watch. As I understand it they were friends when they were younger. Riley's best friends with Liam's little sister, so I'm sure there was some kind of an off-limits vibe there. Anyway, when Liam got out of the Marines and came home and saw Riley for the first time in years, you'd have thought he got hit upside the head with a 2x4. Another little sister she was not."

Tess listened to the play-by-play, breaking up the chicken as it browned. Rock solid foundations that were years old. Both of them. This was what she and Mitch hadn't had time to build.

"Anyway, it all worked out all right in the end."

"Lucky them," she murmured. "Pass the mushrooms."

"How are things going with you and Mitch?"

Tess froze, the cutting board of mushrooms hovering over the skillet. "Why would you think anything's going on between me and Mitch?"

Norah's mouth flexed as if she were trying to hold back a smile. "Well, I might have meant how are things going with you and Mitch and the project, but answering a question with a question to avoid answering makes me think there's a you and Mitch and something else you might want to talk about."

Tess set the cutting board down before she dropped it, trying to fight back the panic. Everything was about to blow up in their faces. "Who else knows?"

"No one. *I* didn't know. Not for sure until just now. You look like you're about to keel over. Come sit down." Norah nudged her onto a bar stool on the other side of the counter and brought over a glass of water. "I didn't intend to upset you. You don't have to talk about this if you don't want to. It's not my business or anyone else's. But I'm here if you need an ear."

Would it be so bad to take Norah into her confidence? All the subterfuge was wearing thin. Tess knew Mitch wanted to tell people about them and was only staying silent in deference to her. The truth was going to come out sooner rather than later anyway, and her gut said she could trust her. Locking her fingers around the glass, she lifted her gaze to Norah's. "We met before I ever came here."

Tess told her about Scotland. Between final instructions for the pasta, the whole story just spilled out, as if a dam had burst. The shock and elation at seeing him again. Worries about the complicated relationship between their families. She stopped shy of talking about the baby, but the rest was enough. By the end of it, she felt somehow lighter, as if she'd purged some of the stress she'd been carrying around.

"Getting a second chance at things has been wonderful, but I haven't had anybody to talk to about this."

Norah propped her chin in her hands. "So why not come clean about being involved?"

"Seriously? You really think that's going to go over well with the rest of the family?"

"I get it. I really do. I was worried about what everyone would think about my being involved with Cam, so we kept it a secret for weeks, and when it came out, it was all this big non-issue."

Tess resisted an urge to press a hand to her belly. "Our situation isn't the same."

"So what are y'all going to do? Keep living together as if you're really just roommates until…what?" Norah asked.

That wasn't an option. Her pants were already starting to get a little tight in the waist. If she ever stopped throwing up and seriously put on weight, the baby bump would be a dead giveaway that things were not simply platonic between them.

"I don't know. We haven't exactly settled on the best means of breaking the news."

"I vote for, 'Hey family, FYI, we're in love with each other. Isn't it great?'" Norah declared.

Tess dropped her gaze. "He hasn't said he's in love with me." Neither had she, but she wasn't going to do anything to prompt him. Over the past couple of weeks, he'd been all about doing anything she needed right now, totally the caretaker. Which was wonderful. But she didn't know if that would extend to saying something he wasn't a hundred percent sure he meant, in the name of her emotional well-being and that of the baby.

Norah made an impatient noise. "Well, I don't know why he's sitting on it because he absolutely is. I've got eyes in my head, and that man is besotted with you."

"How do you know?"

"Because I know Mitch. He's one of my nearest, dearest friends, and I've watched him skirt the edges with woman after woman, always holding something back. But I've never seen him look at another woman the way he looks at you."

Given how long her list of worries was, Tess wished she really could let go of the biggest. "Well, let's hope you're right." Because if she wasn't, Tess didn't know how she was going to cope.

CHAPTER 13

Tears streamed down Tess's cheeks, and her throat ached from crying.

Beside her, Mitch clicked stop on the rolling credits. "You actually *like* this movie? Why?"

She sniffed and sat up, reaching for the box of tissues on the coffee table. "It's a classic, and sometimes you just need a good cry."

"Maybe this is the girl version of needing a good fight to blow off some steam. I feel like I need to marathon all the *Die Hards* to make up for that."

"There are worse ways to spend a Saturday night. I'm game. But I want to go call my mom first." She rose to head upstairs, but Mitch grabbed her hips and pulled her close to press a kiss to her belly.

"Does Eugenia Delphine want popcorn when she comes back?"

"Obi-Wan Kal-el will never turn down popcorn."

His look of adoration was almost, *almost* as good as the words she'd yet to hear. He pressed a kiss to her palm and let her go. "I'll make it and get the movie set up while you chat with your mom."

"I may be a while," Tess warned.

"Take your time."

In their room, she made a nest of pillows and curled up on the bed to dial her mother's number.

"*Ciao, cara!*"

Tess sniffed. "Hey Mamma."

"You've been crying." Maura's voice was threaded through with iron, as if she'd reach through the phone to strangle whoever had upset her daughter.

"*Steel Magnolias*. I just finished watching it, and I was thinking of you. I miss you." Her mother was really the only thing Tess missed about Denver.

Maura sighed. "I love that movie. And I miss you too. How are things in Mississippi?"

"Good. I'm starting on a new project that's going to keep me here a while." Settling in, she told her mom about the small business incubator.

"It's a good direction. I think you'll do well with it. And your father? How is he?"

Tess never knew quite how to answer such questions. Her parents had remained friends since their divorce, but she'd never really known how much of that was a front for her benefit. "He's good. He's happy."

"Good. He hasn't been happy for a long time." The statement had the ring of truth rather than bitterness.

"When *was* he last really happy?"

"All the way happy?" Tess could hear movement and imagined her mother curling up in a similar position on the big white sofa in her living room. "When I was pregnant with you and those first few years after."

Tess sat up, frowning. "Really? But I thought things were kind of rocky between you then. That you were about to break up."

"We were. But when I turned up pregnant, he was elated. I've never seen a man so delighted to be a father. He loved you from the moment he knew you existed." The smile in her mother's voice came over the phone. "And, of course, you know I loved being a mother. That was enough for a long time. Until it wasn't."

Tess felt a ball of dread solidifying in her gut. This wasn't what she'd expected to hear. It wasn't what she *wanted* to hear. She'd needed to believe that she and Mitch were different. That they would overcome their circumstances to make this work. But now that her mother had opened the door, she couldn't not walk through. So she asked the question she'd never been brave enough to pose before. "What really happened with you two?"

Maura was silent for a long time, so long, Tess wasn't sure she was going to answer. "Things just...fizzled. We had passion, your father and I. You came from that. But it wasn't the kind of foundation we needed for the long term."

No proper foundation. Not like the kind of life-long love Judd and Autumn had. Not like any of the crazy-in-love couples she'd met since coming here. She and Mitch had blistering heat and a great deal of affection. And they had this baby. But did they have anything more than that?

As if realizing she'd left the conversation hanging at a low point, Maura continued. "Our lives may not have turned out as we expected, but that was fine. We both got you out of the deal. And you are our greatest treasure."

She was loved. Tess knew and had never doubted that for a moment. But she'd wanted more for both her parents. She wanted more for herself.

"Anyway, I'm glad Gerald's happy. I've never wished him ill."

Maybe not, but Tess remembered the fights at the end. The tears. They always thought they'd hid it well, but she'd known. Maybe they'd gotten past it by now. Her father had moved on, finally. He'd found what he'd been missing. As uncomfortable as that might make Tess, she was happy for him. Now she only wished the same for her mother.

"Are you lonely, Mom?" The question slipped out before she could think better of it, but she didn't pull it back.

"Sometimes. But I wouldn't trade you for the world, *la mia bambina.*"

It made her heart hurt. "I love you too, Mamma." Needing to shift the conversation, Tess forced some cheer into her voice. "So what's going on with you?"

"I'm flying back to Naples at the end of next week to visit my cousins and stay for a while. Your Uncle Gio is talking about opening a vineyard. Can you imagine?" They talked a few more minutes, catching up on that side of the family, but Tess was only partly listening. She was too busy thinking about what her mother had said and wondering how she could've let herself get so caught up in the dream.

Mitch made it easy to trust in the dream. And he meant well. Tess was convinced that he truly believed everything he said. But they weren't going to get the pretty fantasy. They didn't have the foundation, and she didn't come from the same kind of family he did. He would put his all in, just as her father had, and it wouldn't be enough. She wouldn't be enough. It was time for her to accept reality. He'd be a father to their child, but he'd never be truly hers.

"Aren't we going to be way early for family dinner?" Tess asked.

"We didn't have time for me to show you the park when we came out for Cam and Norah's cookout. Since it's still daylight, I thought we'd take the time to do it today." Mitch kept his tone easy, though he had an urge to wipe damp palms on his pants.

Things had been good between them. Better than good. They'd had a couple of weeks to come to terms with their impending parenthood, and the general mood was one of excitement rather than dread. Mitch had to believe that counted for something and that enough time had passed since the initial shock that Tess would really hear what he wanted to tell her. God-willing, there would be announcements at dinner tonight and they could start dealing with the fallout instead of continuing to sneak around. The secrecy was wearing on them both.

He wheeled his truck into a parking space, relieved to see that nobody was out here this late Sunday afternoon. Didn't mean it would stay that way, but as a venue for a proposal, this was a lot less public than the fountain on the green. He hoped he'd get some kind of positive karma for popping the question on the banks of Hope Springs.

Tess straightened in her seat, peering out toward the water. "Oh, it's beautiful."

"Wait 'til you see it up close." Mitch slid out of the driver's side, hustling around to open her door. But, of course, Tess being Tess, she'd already slipped out. He took her hand. "Let's take a little walk."

He gave her a tour of the park proper, relieved to have the privacy to keep her hand tucked in his as he told her about Cam's design.

Tess stroked gentle fingers over the bright blooms of an azalea bush at the edge of the trail. "He's a talented landscape architect. The gardens he put in at The Babylon are a wonder."

"He put in Aunt Sandy's garden when her cancer got bad. He'd read somewhere about the benefits of some nature therapies— that patients had better outcomes if they had ready access to nature. She couldn't leave the house much then, and he wanted her to have something beautiful to look at, somewhere not far to go where she could get out of the house. She's had a helluva good time maintaining it since she went into remission."

"He's a good guy, your cousin. Do you two do much work together?"

"Not as much as I'd like. Other than residential stuff, the majority of my work is on sites elsewhere. I'm fortunate that I can do my job from most anywhere." Mitch knew that might come into play with their future. She played an active role in Peyton Consolidated. He wasn't deluded enough to believe she could necessarily keep doing that from here forever, or that she'd want to.

"Is that how you were able to get away for nearly a month for Europe?"

"Yeah. I took the absolutely necessary stuff with me and fit it in between playing tourist."

"I paid dearly for the week I took in Scotland. Too many irons in the fire. I worked like the devil to catch up when I got back to London."

"Regrets?" He held his breath, waiting for her answer.

She slanted those dark eyes up at him and smiled. "No."

Some of the tension abated. "C'mon. There's something I want to show you." Mitch led her down the trail and into the trees that flanked the bank along this stretch. There was a two-mile loop that doubled back to the parking lot, with benches and overlooks nestled at various intervals. They stopped at one about half a mile in, leaving the trail to stare out over the water.

"This is lovely. It reminds me a little of Loch Faskally, except without the mountains."

"I thought it might. If I'd had my way, I'd have taken you back there for this." It was where he'd first known he wanted to ask her.

"For what?"

Ignoring the suspicion suddenly clouding her eyes, Mitch took her hands and turned to face her, bending to brush a soft kiss across her mouth. After a brief hesitation, she lifted to him. His heart beat like a jackhammer in his chest. What was he afraid of? This was only his everything.

"Tess," he murmured. "My sweet, perfect, Tess. I'm so happy you came into my life."

"Mitch—"

"Just let me get this out, okay?" If he lost his momentum, he was going to botch this again. "I know nothing about us has gone according to plan. We didn't expect to find each other. We didn't expect to get pregnant. We didn't expect to be related in a weird, messy, second marriage sort of way. But even though we didn't have a conventional start, we're going to have an amazing future. I love what that future looks like. I love the family we're making. And I love you. So—" He released one of her hands and dropped to one knee, pulling out the ring that had been burning a hole in his pocket. "—I'm asking you, Teresa Anne Peyton, to be my wife and the mother of my children. Marry me."

As he got through the speech, he finally zeroed in on her face and felt his stomach plummet.

"No." The single syllable was soft. There was no trace of anger or fear, she just seemed decided. Regretful.

Mitch could only stare at her. "I know I flubbed this the first time. It wasn't fair of me to put dictates on you—"

"It's not that. And I'm sorry. I know that's not what you want to hear. I know you believe this is the right thing for this baby. I just...don't."

"How can having two parents in a stable relationship not be the right thing for a child?"

"I'm not going anywhere, Mitch. And I'm not going to do anything to block you from this baby. I want to stay with you. I want to build that life while we keep exploring things between us. But I'm not making any more major life decisions on a whim."

Her words knocked the wind out of him, leaving an ache behind he didn't know how to control. She'd said no. He'd told her he loved her and she didn't say it back. She'd reduced his asking her to marry him to a whim. This was their *life*. The life of their *child*. How could she imagine this was just some kind of rash impulse?

Because he didn't dare open his mouth right now, Mitch stayed silent, struggling to see this from her perspective. He'd learned Tess was a detail-oriented person. A planner to the nth degree. Their affair was the only thing she'd ever done that didn't play to that, and while it led her to him—he didn't doubt her when she said she didn't regret it—it also led her to this unexpected pregnancy, and she was still struggling with that. So, okay, it made sense that she'd be gun-shy about adding to the list of mistakes by breaking pattern again.

But they weren't a mistake, damn it! Their baby wasn't a mistake. And he had no idea where to go from here. How was he supposed to go back to living with her, making all the preparations for this baby, plans for a life together, and *not* want to marry her? He wanted her as his wife. Wanted a proper family. He didn't want to live with her wondering if any day she was going to bolt on him, taking what they'd made between them with her and leaving him with nothing. Again.

Tess looked down at him with wounded eyes. Because she was the one hurt by all of this? Mitch sucked in a breath and rose to his feet, searching for calm. He wasn't about to do anything foolish like starting an argument with his pregnant girlfriend by demanding more explanation before heading to family dinner. Which, Christ, they still had to go to because he couldn't very well call up and cancel on the grounds of a fractured heart, now could he? She needed to avoid any upset, so he would dig deep and find some freaking control.

She wasn't closing the door. She wasn't moving out or breaking up with him. She hadn't said she loved him back, but that wasn't the same as saying she felt nothing. She hadn't denied that there was something between them. He just had to find a way to get her to trust in it. In him. And maybe the only thing that would do that was time. So even though it hurt like a bitch, the only thing he could do right now was accept her rejection and hope like hell she'd come around to the idea in the future.

CHAPTER 14

"*W*e're going to be late for dinner." It was the only thing Mitch said before he turned and headed for the truck.

They were still going to family dinner? How was she supposed to put on a happy face after *this*? How was she supposed to act like everything was fine when things were clearly so very wrong between them? And yet, she didn't want to go straight home with him either. What if he wanted to talk more about all this? She'd already used up almost every shred of control she had not to break down as he got down on one knee and ruined everything. So while dinner would be its own special hell, maybe it would be a stay of execution until she could find a way to hold her shit together.

Tension radiated between them in the cab of the truck. Tess knew she'd hurt him with her refusal. But she absolutely couldn't say yes to this. His proposal had been exactly what she'd feared. All about the baby. Yes, he'd said he'd loved her. Last. As if it was an afterthought he needed to tack on because that's simply what you said when you proposed to a woman. He probably even believed it on some level. But he didn't love her. He loved the idea of her. Of this whole wife and kids and family picture he'd built in his head. A picture that was as alien to her as living on the moon. He wasn't seeing *her* anymore. Ironic, since the entire appeal of an affair with him in the first place was that he had seen *her*, not a Peyton. Now she'd been lost again, under the umbrella of something else. All he could see was the mother of his child, not just Tess. Maybe she was doomed never to find anyone who could love her simply for her.

Mitch parked the truck behind the long row of vehicles in Cam and Norah's driveway. For a long moment neither of them spoke, simply looking straight ahead.

"We can leave whenever you're ready." He still didn't look at her.

"Okay."

By the time they made it to the door, they'd both put on their *everything's fine* faces. She stepped into the usual chaos of Campbells, saying her hellos and numbly giving and accepting hugs. Mitch didn't stick close. They didn't touch, and for once that was okay. There wouldn't be any of the lingering glances that always threatened to give them away. He needed some space from her. She understood that. She could use a little from him, too. Maybe she'd get a room at The Babylon again for a while, until they'd come back to some sort of even keel.

Trey carried over a glass of wine. "We are celebrating! The purchase of the factory has officially gone through."

Tess accepted the glass but didn't actually drink. The scent of alcohol was sharp in her nose. "That's great, Dad. I'll get Brody out to the site next week to see whether he can work us into the schedule."

"I know he's booked up a while, but we can afford to wait a little for the sake of working with someone we trust."

Waiting. Being here longer without any real action. With everything else weighing heavy on her heart, Tess wasn't sure how long she could stand it. As everyone around her continued to chatter away about her brainchild, she could barely keep up with the conversation. Restless, uncertain, she spun the glass by the stem.

What was going to happen now? Was Mitch going to be okay accepting the status quo? She'd thought she handled the situation as well as she could. She didn't want anything else to change. But what if she'd lost whatever chance she had with him by not being willing to meet him on his terms? The idea of it sent a flare of anger and frustration scorching through the hurt. How could he box her in like this? She'd had to face so much adjustment in such a short span of time. It wasn't fair for him to throw this at her too and expect her to just jump at it. Didn't he understand that?

Of course he didn't. Because he hadn't truly had time to know her. Not all the way.

"Okay everybody, dinner is ready," Norah announced. "Head to the dining room."

Tess automatically began moving down the hall. "What are we having?" She could talk about food. Food was normal. She desperately needed some normal.

"I found this recipe for pork chops with tomato curry I've been dying to try."

"I ate tons of curry while I lived in London. It became a real favorite."

"This one intrigued me." Norah leaned over the table and lifted the lid on a large dish.

The pungent scent struck Tess like a blow. Her body jerked in defense as her gag reflex kicked in at Incredible Hulk strength. She barely managed to set down the wine before sprinting down the hall for the powder room. She couldn't even get the door closed before she hit her knees and vomited up everything in her stomach.

Moments later familiar, gentle hands pulled back her hair. Mitch. Because of course. He efficiently wet a cloth at the sink with one hand as he continued to hold her hair through the second round—because her stomach was never satisfied with just one. It was a routine they'd perfected. But she just couldn't take it right now. This man was the reason her life, her body had spun completely out of control. So as soon as she found the strength, she smacked his hand away. "For God's sake, Mitch, I'm pregnant, not an invalid. Leave me be."

The hand curled at her nape in a gesture of comfort froze and withdrew.

Guilt immediately washed over her. She was upset, confused, but he was only being kind and supportive. She dropped to her butt and turned, intending to apologize...and saw her father standing in the hallway behind him, his jaw slack with shock.

Tess dropped her head against her updrawn knees. "Shit."

"Pregnant?" Trey's shocked stutter from the hall had Mitch closing his eyes.

She was supposed to have said yes. They were supposed to announce their engagement and give everybody a little while to get used to the idea of the two of them as a couple before they sprang the news of the baby. But she'd said no, and now the secret was out with no preparation, no forethought, no means of damage control. Absolutely nothing was going the way it was supposed to. Could this day get any worse?

No. Mitch knew better than to ask that question. Everything could always get worse.

Knowing it probably would before this was over—especially for Tess—he backed out of the bathroom. No matter how frustrated he was right now, he'd do whatever he could to shield her from the backlash.

"Take however much time you need." He shut the door and braced himself. He'd never dreaded facing his family before, but he dreaded this. What would they say? What would they do?

Didn't matter. Mitch turned to find all of them trailing down the hall in a line, staring with various degrees of shock and confusion.

Trey's mouth opened and closed like a fish. "Did she say pregnant?"

Mitch kept his tone even, quiet. "Everybody go sit down."

Nobody moved other than to split their stares between him and the door at his back. Beyond the door, the toilet flushed and the water turned on.

He crossed his arms and drew himself up to his full height. Bodyguard wasn't his default role, but he sure as hell wasn't going to allow them to make Tess feel any worse about this. "She's been through enough without having the lot of you staring at her like she's a circus freak. Sit the hell down."

The steel in his tone earned him several sharp looks, especially from the older generations, but they started moving, filing into the living room. Nobody went into the dining room except Norah, probably to cover the food again.

The hallway was empty by the time the door opened and Tess emerged. She'd found some composure again, wrapping herself in a determined dignity, despite the fact she'd been puking her guts up just minutes ago. It was a helluva trick. She didn't meet his eyes as she moved down the hall, toward the murmuring voices. Mitch was right behind. Everybody fell to silence as they came into the room.

Tess zeroed in on her dad, head held high, almost defiant. "Yes, I said I'm pregnant."

"How far?"

"A little over eleven weeks."

A muscle jumped in his jaw, and Sandy reached over to lay a hand on his arm as he ground out, "Who?"

Some of Tess's defiance wavered and she swallowed. Mitch wrapped his arm around her stiff shoulders, unsurprised when she didn't tuck into him. God forbid she let him take care of her here, even now. But he held his ground as exclamations of shock rippled through the room. Trey's hands had balled to fists, and Mitch couldn't even look at his own parents.

"We met in Edinburgh. She's why I extended my trip."

It took the group approximately three seconds to do the math and conclude they'd fallen into bed almost as soon as they met. Which wasn't inaccurate but was uncomfortable as hell as the realization settled in.

Trey scooped a hand through his hair. "I don't even know what to say about this."

Tess's back went ramrod straight as she took a step toward him. "You don't get to say a damned thing to me about this. You don't get to judge. We both know I wouldn't be here right now if not for this exact situation."

Mitch absorbed that kick to his gut. He'd wanted her from the first, before the baby. Without the baby. Was she really saying she wouldn't be with him at all if not for it?

Maybe he had it wrong. She was strung out and upset and embarrassed, no doubt feeling cornered by having things come out like this. He had to believe she meant something else.

A vein in Trey's temple began to throb in time with the muscle tick in his jaw. "Will you be getting married?"

"Of course you would ask that," she scoffed.

"It's a relevant question."

"A baby is a terrible reason to get married."

At the end of his rope, needing answers, Mitch turned toward her. "Why? You've said no, but you haven't explained why. It's the right thing to do. You're carrying *my child.*"

She flinched at the words, as if he'd lobbed some terrible insult. But before he could process the reaction, she squared off with him and lifted her eyes to his. "Because you don't love me."

His head kicked back as if she'd punched him. "Tess." After everything they'd shared, how could she believe that? "Did you hear anything I said to you this afternoon?"

"Every word. You love this baby. I have absolutely no doubt

about that. And you've tangled that up with what you feel for me. But the truth is, you don't know me well enough to love me. How could you? That wasn't what any of this was supposed to be about. God knows, that wasn't what either of us was looking for when we started this."

"Don't," he growled. "Don't reduce this to a casual affair. We were more than we intended from the start, and you know it."

"Maybe we could have been."

The past tense and her expression of absolute resignation and regret had Mitch's gut clenching in panicked desperation.

Tess laid a hand over her belly. "But this...this changed everything."

"Why?" he demanded. For the life of him he couldn't understand where this defeatist attitude was coming from. Maybe the baby upped the timetable. And sure, it added a layer of stress they otherwise wouldn't have had. But it didn't change how they felt about each other.

The breath she sucked in was slow and measured, as if she was searching for patience—or maybe the words to explain the concept to a two year old. "You don't understand. Of course you don't. You come from *this*." She gestured to the room at large. To his family, who still looked on in shock. "You can't fathom any other way to be. I can't even begin to tell you how envious I am that you can take that for granted. That the idea of a perfect, multi-generational family, with two point five kids and a sloppy dog is a foregone conclusion for you. But that's not what would happen with us."

"Why the hell not?"

"You'd marry me out of obligation and some twisted, old-fashioned sense of nobility. And for a while, it would be fine. But eventually the heat that brought us together in the first place will burn out. Until there's nothing left but ash and a resentment that will block out everything but the dimmest memories of anything that was ever good between us. I won't go through that with you. I can't. I deserve more than that. And so do you. So I'm saving us both from the prison of your convictions."

A prison of my convictions.

The words hit Mitch like bullets, one after another. He half expected to see blood soaking the front of his shirt, but he couldn't look away from her because he understood that if he lost this connection with her now, he'd lose *her*.

He couldn't even begin to imagine the harsh future she painted. Everything in him rejected it. Though her body language shouted *hands off*, he reached for her, curling his hands around her shoulders to keep her from pulling away any further. "That's *one* possible outcome. Why are you so damned certain that's how it would be?"

She trembled under his touch, her eyes full of unshed tears. For one second, Mitch thought she'd step into him. Instead she wrenched free, her hands balling to fists, her jaw firming. "Because I lived it. *That* is the foundation *I* come from. It's no kind of environment to raise a child in, and I won't do it to mine. Don't ask me to."

Stunned, Mitch could only stare as her tears erupted.

"Tess—" Trey's voice was strained.

She stumbled back, raising both her hands as if to ward off a blow. "Don't! Just—don't." She backpedaled, edging toward the door. "I have to go." It only took her two steps to stop, apparently remembering she'd ridden with him. Panic flashed over her face.

Mitch stepped toward her, understanding only that she needed to get the hell out of here. "We'll go."

"No. I can't—I just can't."

"Take my car." Cecily pressed keys into Tess's hand.

Tess's broken whisper of thanks simply gutted him. He took another step toward her only to find his path blocked by Cam.

"Let her go, man."

"She's not in any shape to drive," Mitch insisted, feeling the panic rise as she disappeared around the corner, into the hall.

Ethan broke away. "I'll follow to make sure she gets home okay."

But Mitch barely heard the promise over the sound of the front door closing, as the woman he loved ran away from him.

Again.

CHAPTER 15

"Is there anything else we can do for you, Miss Peyton?" There was such concern and sympathy in the receptionist's eyes as Tess checked back into The Babylon.

For maybe the first time in her life, Tess knew she wasn't dignified and she sure as hell wasn't living up to the family name. Her eyes were red-rimmed and swollen. She'd been sobbing since she left family dinner, all through the drive back to the house to pack up her stuff. She'd swapped to her own car, sent a text to Cecily in thanks, and retreated before Mitch could get home. Given he didn't interrupt her, someone had probably detained him. She'd owe them a thank you, too.

"No, thank you." Half-blind with the fresh bout of tears gathering in her eyes, Tess took the key card and headed for the elevator. It stayed blessedly empty as she went up to the penthouse.

As soon as she shut the door to her room, she dropped her bags and sank to the floor, back against the entryway wall.

Everything was so damned wrong. Broken. What had been full of such promise had shattered, and there was no hope of putting it back together again. Or maybe that was her heart. Why couldn't he have waited? Why did he have to force the issue? Why couldn't they have had more time to figure all this out?

It hardly mattered now. For once, there was no amount of work, no amount of Peyton stubbornness or dedication that would get her what she wanted. She couldn't make Mitch love her the way she needed. And she couldn't take this baby out of the equation. Wouldn't, even if she could. Would she ultimately find solace in being a parent, in loving this child with everything inside her, the way her mother had?

The knock on the door had her jolting. She didn't want to see anybody, not even the freaking bellboy. But she dragged herself to her feet and peered through the peephole. Her father stood on the other side. Not a surprise. She didn't really think she could run away after dropping the bomb of her pregnancy. He'd expect explanations. On a sigh she flattened her hands and pressed her brow against the door. At least it wasn't Mitch. For a few moments, she considered ignoring him. But given he owned the hotel, if he wanted in, he'd find a way in.

She opened the door and caught the flash of relief before he took in the sight of her.

"Oh, sweetheart."

Tess stepped back, figuring the best defense was a good offense. "I know I'm a screwup, and this whole pregnancy will impact my ability to travel hither and yon to do my job, so if we could maybe skip over the interrogation or lecture on how you're so disappointed, that would be great. Because I really can't take any more today."

He stepped through the door and wrapped her in a tight hug. "I'm sorry. I'm so sorry for how I reacted. It was just such a shock. You are *not* a screw up. I'm not disappointed in you, and the job's not going anywhere."

Her throat strained against the knot of tears even as relief had her burrowing in, hanging on tight. At least she hadn't screwed up her entire life.

Trey pressed his cheek to her hair. "You can keep doing whatever you want, whether that's continuing to oversee the development of the small business incubator here or going back to Denver."

"I don't know what I want."

"You don't have to decide right now. Come on. Let's go sit down."

He settled her on the sofa and tucked a throw around her. Absurd that she was freezing in May in Mississippi. But she tugged the blanket tighter, as if it would somehow protect her from the consequences of the mess she was in.

A minute later, Trey came back with a glass of water. "Here, drink this now."

Obedient, she swallowed it down, knowing it wouldn't be enough to dent the dehydration headache that was barreling toward a migraine.

Her dad sank down on the other end of the couch and tucked her feet into his lap. "So you and Mitch."

Just hearing their names linked had a fresh wave of tears streaming down her face. "I don't think there is any more me and Mitch after this." She'd done a helluva job making sure of that, hadn't she?

"Do you love him?"

Miserable, she clutched a pillow to her chest. "Does it matter?"

"Well, you're going to be in each other's lives on a permanent basis either way, so I'd say it does."

Tess swallowed. "Yeah, yeah I do. So much. He's a good man. That's not in question or I'd never have been with him to begin with. I just…for once I wanted to be enough. Just me."

Trey frowned. "Why wouldn't you think you are?"

"He doesn't see anything but this baby. No one should ever use a child as the glue for a marriage."

Pain flashed over his features. "Is that really what you think your mom and I did?"

"I know it's what you did. And it didn't work. I literally watched you fall apart over the course of years. Because I wasn't enough."

"Oh, honey." He reached out to skim a hand over her cheek. "The reason our marriage fell apart had nothing to do with you."

"You were going to break up before Mom turned up pregnant."

"We'd talked about it. Because I was still in love with Sandy."

Tess lowered the pillow. "Like, your current wife, Sandy?"

"Yeah."

"I don't understand."

He settled back against the cushions, obviously bracing himself for this story. "You know your mother and I met at the University of Washington. What I never told you was that I didn't start there. I was at Ole Miss for my first two years of college. That's where Sandy and I met."

"You knew her in college?"

"Yeah. We were friends. Couldn't be more than that because she was already married to her high school sweetheart. But that didn't stop me from falling in love with her or her with me."

"Did you have an affair?"

"No. We never crossed that line. Her husband was an ass. Immature, selfish. She decided to leave him. We had this whole big plan to get her away, start divorce proceedings. When she didn't show at our meeting place, I went to find her. I thought maybe Waylan had come home to find her packing and stopped her from leaving. I saw her with him through the window, and it looked like they were reconciling, like she'd chosen him. So I left, without a word. Without getting closure. And damn if that didn't stick with me. For years. If I'd known what was really going on…" He trailed off, shaking his head. "Doesn't matter. What I need you to know, to really understand, is that your mother and I didn't break up because you weren't a strong enough glue."

"You were in love with someone else."

"Yeah. Always have been, even if it took me years to admit it.

When I married Maura, I was truly trying to move on. We had passion and affection and respect. Plenty of marriages turn into more from less than that."

"I won't settle for less." It seemed she was an all or nothing sort of woman.

"That's your decision. And I support you in it, whatever you choose. But be clear on this: My relationship with your mother failed because my heart wasn't in it a hundred percent. It had nothing to do with us suddenly becoming parents before we were ready, before we'd figured things out. This baby—*your* baby—is not an automatic death sentence to whatever is between you and Mitch. It's not a guarantee that you two will turn out like your mother and I did."

Tess clung to the pillow, as if that was somehow going to stop the dizzy spin of her world realigning. With this one detail, he'd just rewritten the story of her life. She couldn't get her head around it.

Was he right? Was there still some kind of a chance for the two of them to salvage their relationship? Tess wanted to believe him. Was desperate to cling to any shred of possibility that things weren't destroyed. But she was so very afraid.

Shifting, she crawled into his lap, curling up as she hadn't since she was a little girl, so her head was tucked against his shoulder. "I hope you're right."

Her father held her for a long time, stroking her back. "I do have one thing to ask of you in all this."

Tess tensed. *Please don't ask for more details about how we got together.* "What?"

"Can we come up with some other name for me than Grandpa? I just don't feel that old."

And though her heart was broken, she managed to find a laugh.

∾

SHE WAS GONE.

Mitch had known that when he saw her car wasn't in the garage, but he'd torn through the house anyway, hoping to find something—anything—to prove him wrong. He dropped down onto the bed in the suite down the hall from their room, staring into the closet. Some of her things were still there, but the suitcase and most of the clothes weren't. Several hangers lay strewn on the floor, as if she hadn't been able to get out fast enough to take care in packing. He shouldn't have been surprised that she hadn't stuck around to work through all of this. Bolting was a thing she did. He knew that from first-hand experience. She'd been scared of what she felt in Scotland. It had been far more than fear he'd seen in her face today. It had been utter devastation.

He could relate. The foundation of his world felt cracked, and he was terrified it couldn't be mended. But all of his own agony and frustration was secondary for the moment. Because Tess was out there, scared and upset and behind the wheel. It wasn't safe. And beyond the worry that she'd get into an accident, he had no way of knowing whether she was, even now, on the way to the airport to meet the company's private jet to walk out of his life forever.

She'd told him she wasn't going to do anything to keep him from their baby. But she'd also said she wanted to stay and keep exploring things between them and here she was gone, without a word, without a note. Again. So, no, he wouldn't put it past her to run far and fast because apparently her fear was bigger than anything she felt for him.

You don't love me.

The look on her face...the utter heartbreak. Mitch still couldn't get over the fact that she truly didn't believe him. He'd spelled it out, and she'd heard none of it. How the hell was he supposed to combat that?

Where the hell was she so he could try?

The doorbell rang. Mitch bolted down the stairs. But, of course, it wasn't Tess. Aunt Sandy stood on his front stoop. Maybe she was here to browbeat him over his involvement with Tess in the first place. Taking over that duty for her husband? Or maybe for his own parents because they were too ashamed of him they couldn't even ream him in person. He didn't really want to open the door to any of that. But maybe she had news about Tess. He needed that more than he needed to protect himself from recriminations.

"She's at The Babylon."

Mitch's hand flexed on the open door. So she wasn't driving and she hadn't left town. Yet. But was it only a matter of time? Until she could make the necessary arrangements?

He'd worry about that later. For now, he let go of the fear and worry over her safety and let all his own hurt and frustration come to a boil. How the hell had his life gotten to be such a damned mess?

"Thanks for letting me know." He started to shut the door, but his aunt blocked it.

"I'm not finished."

"Are you here to lecture me for daring to put my hands on her? For making the family awkward? Because I swear to God, I had no idea who she was when we met, and it wasn't my idea to keep us a secret."

"No. I'm here to give you some perspective."

Well, that was just fucking peachy.

But he backed up to let her in. Figuring he'd need it for whatever was coming, Mitch headed to the sideboard in the dining room and poured himself a generous glass of bourbon.

"Sit." The single word held all the authority she'd once wielded as the high school principal.

Mitch found himself sitting, though more from dread than intimidation.

"What has Tess told you about her parents?"

"Not a lot. We talked about Trey some. A little about her mom. It wasn't something we discussed really."

"You know they're divorced. Have been for years."

"Sure. But I don't know why she thinks that's the automatic outcome here."

"Probably because there are a lot of similarities between your situation and that of her parents."

"What? They had a vacation fling and got pregnant?" He said it with sarcasm, but stopped with the glass halfway to his mouth when he caught her level stare.

"Not vacation fling, no. Trey and Maura dated for more than a year. But yes, she got pregnant, and they got married."

Mitch sipped his bourbon and let that sink in. So when she'd said she wouldn't be here if not for this exact situation, she'd meant she literally wouldn't exist. That hadn't been a slap at him, but at her father. Who had instantly asked if they were getting married.

I'm saving us both from the prison of your convictions.

"They only got married because of her," he realized.

"Not entirely, but mostly. Chances are, the relationship would have fizzled out if left to run its course."

But it hadn't been left to run its course. They'd gone with convention, gotten married, and as the child of that union, Tess had been a first-hand witness to the fallout.

Eventually the heat that brought us together in the first place will burn out. Until there's nothing left but ash and a resentment that will block out everything but the dimmest memories of anything that was ever good between us.

Jesus. Was that what her parents had been like growing up? The aftermath of some kind of cold war? It was so far from his own experience, with that multi-generational family and the sloppy dog, Mitch couldn't even wrap his head around it. But he was beginning to understand what vastly different backgrounds they came from.

"I thought she was worried the baby would change things because she didn't think I was okay with being a father. I was trying to make her see that I'm totally on board with the whole package, and instead I made her think the package was the only thing I cared about." Because saying marriage was the right thing put him in the same boat as her father and made everything about the baby. Exactly what he'd wanted to avoid.

"Probably. Their divorce was extremely hard on her, obviously harder even than Trey realized. And she saw more than they meant for her to. That's what she comes from. She doesn't have all the examples of solid relationships you have, so she doesn't know how to trust you when you say that everything will turn out all right in the end. For her family, it didn't."

Mitch tossed back the rest of the bourbon, feeling a little clarity come with the burn of the alcohol. "I think she's afraid of us. Our whole family and way of life. I'd thought it was just her being weirded out and not knowing how to act around you as his second wife, but she's outright terrified of what we represent."

"Maybe. For someone like her, our family is a bit like a fairy tale."

"She deserves the fairy tale."

"Can you give it to her?"

He wanted to do that more than anything. Because she was his fairy tale, too. "I'm sure as hell trying. But she thinks my loving her is only because of the baby."

"Is it?"

"No. Maybe my feelings got deeper, faster because of the baby, but I loved her before I ever knew what we'd made."

"Then find a way to make her see she's enough."

CHAPTER 16

*T*ess's whole body ached. Probably because she'd cried out every remaining ounce of fluid after her father left. Then she'd forced herself to guzzle more water, thinking dehydration was probably bad for the baby. She'd caught only snatches of sleep, and those had been full of Mitch and his agonized expression as she'd run from him.

Coward.

The echo of the accusation was still with her as she crawled out of bed just after the sun. And why shouldn't it be? She was a coward, too terrified to face him and lay her heart bare, lest it not be enough.

Uncomfortable with the truth of it, Tess forced herself straight into work. The job had always been her salvation, the place she was in control. After the past few weeks, she needed to be in control of *something*. But after following up on the Picadilly project with her crew in London, she couldn't seem to find enough focus for anything else. The incubator was on hold until Brody called to schedule the walk-through, and she wasn't in any shape to get involved in anything else.

Mitch hadn't called or come by. And what did she expect?

She'd run. How many times could she leave this man behind and expect him to still want to follow? She'd wanted—needed—space after the debacle of that family dinner. But distance hadn't made her feel any better and sure as hell hadn't brought any clarity.

Because she had no idea what else to do, Tess upended the suitcase on her bed and began to methodically smooth and fold, repacking the stuff she'd just thrown into the bag last night. She recognized it for the false sense of order it was but continued the familiar ritual because she needed to control *something*, anything, no matter how small.

At the knock on the penthouse door, she dropped the blouse she was folding.

Mitch.

Her heart leapt, even as her feet closed the distance and her hand closed over the knob.

It wasn't Mitch.

It was an army of Campbell women. Sandy, Norah, Cecily, Miranda, Grammy, Anita, and even Mitch's mother were all crowded in the hall. What the hell were they all doing here?

Only a lifetime of etiquette lessons kept her from simply shutting the door in their faces and hiding.

"We're sorry to disturb you," Norah began.

"No we're not," Miranda said. "We need to talk to you." She didn't wait for an invitation before edging her way into the penthouse.

"Please, come in," Tess muttered.

Liz heaved a sigh as she followed. "I swear she wasn't raised in a barn."

Knowing there'd be no getting rid of them until they'd said whatever it was they came here to say, Tess stepped back to open the door fully. Once they'd all filed inside, she shut it and fell into hostess mode. "Can I offer you coffee or tea?"

What am I doing? I don't want them to stay.

"There's no need to go to any trouble," Sandy said.

An awkward silence draped over the room. Tess couldn't resist the compulsion to fill it. "I'm sorry for the...scene...yesterday."

Grammy waved that off. "Oh honey, if we didn't have a spectacle once a month, something would be wrong."

What the hell was she supposed to say to that? Tess dug deep, trying to find some kind of normal something she could fall back on, but it was simply beyond her just now. "If you're here to plead Mitch's case—"

"No. We're here to support you," Sandy said.

"I—what?"

"Let me start, because if this kumbaya session runs long, I've got to get to the clinic to open." Miranda crossed her arms. "Yesterday was incredibly difficult for you, and we want to apologize collectively if we made it worse."

"I'm reasonably sure I did that all by myself."

Miranda's face softened with sympathy. "My bone-headed brother helped."

"He's not bone-headed," Tess snapped. "He's kind and honorable and loyal to a fault."

Her lips twitched. "So you are in love with him."

"Miranda," Norah warned.

"She doesn't have to answer. It's written all over her face."

Liz reached out, as if she wanted to touch Tess, but folded her hands instead. "You're right. My son is all of those things, but he's also old-fashioned, chivalrous, and very thick-headed. He has in his head that there is one right way to do things and he didn't listen to you like he should have."

"The fact of the matter is, marriage isn't always the right thing in these situations. That you're willing to stand up to that says a great deal about your character," Sandy said. "I wasn't that strong when I found out I was pregnant the same day I was planning to leave my first husband for Trey. I opted to stay, because I was afraid of the alternative. I lost a lot of years with your father. I can't say it was the wrong choice because if I'd gone to him like we'd planned, there'd be no you. But I absolutely agree with you that a baby is not a good basis for a marriage. It didn't save mine."

It looked like they were reconciling, like she'd chosen him. So I left, without a word.

Her father's words echoed in her head. This was what he hadn't known. Sandy hadn't chosen her husband, she'd chosen her son. Tess thought about what her dad had said about Sandy's first husband—Immature. Selfish. An ass—and she felt a pang for what Sandy had no doubt endured because of that choice. Mitch was none of those things. They didn't need saving from being a poor match in the first place. And he wasn't like her father, either. There was no other woman with a claim on his affections. So maybe they had a stronger foundation than she'd given them credit for.

Tess studied this woman who'd held her father's heart for decades. "With respect, Dad's told me some about your ex-husband. If you're comparing Mitch to him on any level, I'm going to have to ask you to leave."

"Oh, she'll fit into the family just fine," Grammy crowed in satisfaction.

"She hasn't agreed to marry him," Anita pointed out.

"And she doesn't have to," Norah added. "That baby is a Campbell either way, and that makes Tess family."

This time Liz did reach out, stroking a hand down Tess's arm. "Whatever you choose, he'll be a good father."

"I know he will. That's never been a question." This child was already loved. By its father and the rest of his insanely tight-knit family. And Tess understood, as they all pulled her in for hugs, that they'd be there for her and this baby, no matter what happened with her and Mitch. That kind of love was more than a little heartbreaking because she wanted it so much for herself.

When they'd gone, she sank down on the sofa, wondering for the first time if maybe she wasn't being fair to Mitch. From her front-row seat to the failing of her parents' marriage, she'd learned to expect the worst out of this situation. And yet, at every turn, his upbringing had prepared him to expect the opposite. They couldn't both be right.

Never in her life had Tess wanted so desperately to be wrong.

I'll never know if I don't try.

Her purse and keys were already in her hands when the phone rang. She fished it out, seeing Brody's name flashing on the screen.

"This is Tess."

"Hey, my client meeting got cancelled this morning, so I find myself with time to go over the site plans. Are you free?"

She wanted to say no. She wanted to get in her car and go straight over to the house to see if she could fix what was broken between them. But Brody's call reminded her that it was, in fact, a work day, and she had a job to do.

"I can meet you over there in fifteen minutes."

She headed to her car on autopilot, sifting through the everyday details she'd put out of her mind when everything had blown up yesterday. Mitch had a meeting in Lawley this morning, so he probably wasn't even home. Even as disappointment flared, she squashed it. The extra time was okay. Maybe by the time he got back, she'd have figured out what she needed to say.

I love you.

That needed to be right at the top. She'd been so worried about whether he did or could love her, she hadn't ever told him how she felt. What if he felt as lost and rejected as she did? The idea that she could've hurt him like that made her ill. Or more ill than she already was. By the time she'd fought off the fresh wave of nausea, she'd overshot her turn. Pulling into a rutted track past the chainlink fence, she opened the door and vomited. Again.

Dear Lord, would this baby ever let her keep food down?

Weak and shaky, she shut the door and leaned her head back against the seat. She'd just sit here for a few minutes with her eyes closed until it passed.

Something struck the car. Her body whipped with the impact of the crash. Before she could even scream, before the airbag deployed and the seatbelt dug deep, driving the air from her lungs, Tess's head cracked against the window and she slid into blackness.

~

HEART IN HIS THROAT, Mitch bolted toward the ER from the hospital parking lot. He hadn't been able to breathe since he got the call that Tess had been in an accident. That had been forty-five minutes ago, and he still knew nothing other than the ambulance had rushed her to the hospital. He'd floored his gas pedal as he raced back from Lawley, sending disjointed prayers up to the Almighty that she just be okay.

He burst through the automatic doors into the ER, practically crashing into the reception desk. "Tess Peyton. Where is she? What's going on?"

The nurse on duty wasn't familiar. Her no-nonsense expression didn't shift as she fixed steely blue eyes on him. "Sir, I'm going to need you to calm down."

Calm down? How the fuck was he supposed to be calm when he knew *nothing*, not even whether Tess was alive or dead? Curling his hands around the edges of the counter, Mitch struggled to keep some of the panic out of his voice. "Teresa Anne Peyton was brought in about an hour ago. Car accident. She's pregnant. I need to know what's going on."

"Are you family?"

"She's the mother of my child." Tess would hate being reduced to that, but what else could he say after last night?

The woman's fingers tapped at a keyboard in a slow hunt and peck. How the hell could someone who worked with computers not know how to type? Before he could take off the nurse's head for not being faster, someone called his name.

Sandy crossed the industrial tile floor, her heels echoing in the mostly empty space. His parents, Grammy, Cecily, Cam, and Norah took up one corner. God, was this an all-hands-on-deck sort of vigil?

Mitch abandoned the front desk. "Where is she? Is she all right?"

"She's stable."

Stable. That wasn't the same as all right.

His knees wobbled and his stomach bottomed out. He was too afraid to ask about the baby. "What the hell happened?"

"She was on her way to meet Brody out at the job site. Her car was hit. The other driver was texting."

Rage washed his vision red. Her life, the life of his child, were in danger because some *asshole* couldn't wait to get where he was going. "How bad?" He gritted out the words as he clenched and unclenched his fists.

"They're still running tests. Trey's back with her now."

Even as she spoke, the double doors leading back to the patient areas opened and Trey came through. Mitch made it over to the other man in three strides, scanning his face for the answers he so desperately needed. Stress, but no terror or grief. That was probably a good sign, right?

"She's okay."

Words weren't enough. "I have to see her." He needed to touch her. Needed real, verified proof that she was going to be fine.

Mitch started to push past him, to catch the door that hadn't quite swung shut, but Trey slapped a hand against his chest. "You need to calm the hell down. The last thing she needs right now is to see you upset. Can you do that?"

He felt like he was flying apart as all the fear and worry and anger coalesced inside him. But he'd do whatever had to be done to get to Tess, so he simply nodded and obediently followed the other man into the labyrinth behind the doors.

Outside her room, Trey stopped him. "She looks a little rough. It's important that you keep your head. Got it?"

Mitch nodded and took several breaths to brace himself before easing into the room.

Tess lay in a hospital bed, eyes closed. An ugly bruise at her temple was bisected by a white swatch of bandage. More bruises and abrasions were visible where the hospital gown had slipped off her shoulder. From the seatbelt, probably. An assortment of monitors beeped with steady rhythms, but there was no oxygen, no IV. That was good, right?

Mitch stepped closer, his feet scuffing on the tile, and she opened her eyes. Relief flashed across her face, and that unguarded emotion had him crossing the room, taking her hand.

Her fingers curled tight in his and held on. "Hi."

"You scared ten years off my life. Are you okay?"

"I've felt better. I've got a concussion, and I'm banged up pretty good, but they tell me nothing's broken. My blood pressure is up and they're checking a few more things, but I'm going to be fine."

Mitch exhaled and reached to drag over a chair-because his knees weren't altogether steady. He pressed their joined hands to his cheek. "Thank God. And—" His gaze dropped, at last, to her belly.

"They're still running tests, but the heartbeat is good and there's no sign of bleeding. No cramping."

The last of the fear let go its stranglehold on his chest. Overwhelmed with relief and gratitude, he pressed his face to the bed. "I thought I'd lost you."

Her fingers stroked the back of his hand. "There was a minute there I thought the same. I was so scared I wouldn't get a chance to say that I'm sorry."

He turned his face toward her, catching the clear regret in her dark eyes and feeling the first kindle of renewed hope. "For what?"

"For running away. For being so afraid and not telling you *why*."

"I should have seen that you were scared. I should have asked."

Her mouth quirked. "Seen how? With your super-secret mind-reading powers?"

"I know you."

"On a lot of levels you do. But not totally, and that's got nothing to do with how you feel about me and everything to do with time. We simply haven't had that much of it together, and what we have wasn't focused on that. There were so many points I could have explained about my parents, but it's not a thing I talk about. It wasn't even something I even consciously thought about until I got here and came face-to-face with your family."

"We freak you out." At her start of surprise he shrugged. "Like I said. I know you."

"You're right. They do freak me out. I don't know how to be a part of that."

Not knowing how to be a part of something wasn't the same as not wanting to be part of it. Clinging to that, to her, he straightened. "Well, you've met them, right? It's not like they collectively give you much choice. We just kind of absorb people and make them ours."

That almost got a smile out of her. "I'm starting to get that."

"You're one of ours, Tess."

The smile dimmed. "Because of Dad. Because of this baby." She laid a protective hand over her stomach.

"Because I love you."

She opened her mouth, probably to argue with him, but he pressed on. "I know you don't trust that. I know you think it's only because of the baby. But it's not." And suddenly he knew exactly how to prove it. He pulled out his wallet, digging through until he found what he wanted. "Look at this."

∽

TESS TOOK the paper and unfolded it. "What is this?"

"The receipt for your engagement ring."

Horrified, she stared at him. "Please tell me you don't think I'm the kind of woman who cares about how much something cost."

"Look at the date, Tess."

She dropped her gaze, skimming the receipt for the transaction date. February 29th. From a jeweler in Pitlochry. Tess went very still, even as the monitor began to broadcast the wild beating of her heart. "You bought an engagement ring after *four days?*"

"I did."

"That's crazy. Why would you do that? You didn't even know my last name."

"Because it was Leap Day and I decided to take a leap." He scooted closer, folding her hands back in his. "I screwed this up royally, both times. I get that. What I *should* have said at the lake yesterday was this: I love you. I think I did almost from the first moment I saw you up on that stage, so vivid and vibrant and unapologetically you. And every minute we spent together that week just further solidified for me that I wanted you in my life for every day. It didn't matter that we hadn't known each other that long or that your life was there and mine was here. It didn't even matter that I didn't know your full name. I knew *you*. And I loved you. So I bought that ring and I bided my time because even though I knew beyond a shadow of a doubt, I figured you'd be a harder sell and I wanted to give you more time. That last day, I planned to take you back to Loch Faskally and ask you to marry me. I knew it was insane and crazy, and yet I knew if I didn't, I'd regret it. But I didn't get the chance because you bolted."

Tess dropped her gaze, fresh tears gathering in her eyes. She'd run from him because she hadn't trusted him, hadn't trusted herself. And it seemed in the past couple months she'd learned nothing.

Mitch cupped the uninjured side of her face and tipped her head up to meet his gaze. "No, don't beat yourself up for that. It is what it is. You were scared. So was I. But we got this second chance. And I was beyond grateful that the Universe hadn't abandoned us. Then the baby happened and it just felt like icing on the world's most perfect cake. I love our child. I love the life we can all have together, on whatever terms you're comfortable with. But I need you to know, I loved you first. Before all of it. And I didn't say it because I didn't want to scare you, but that sure as hell blew up in my face, so I'm saying it now. I love you. And I'll say it every day for the rest of forever, if you'll let me. I'll say it as often as you need, do whatever I can to show you until you really, truly believe me. I love you, and I want to build a life with you, Tess. Whether it's here or in Denver or Timbuktu. I want to marry you. Whenever you want. Whether that's tomorrow or after the baby's born. I just need you."

It was everything she'd needed to hear. He loved her. Really, truly loved *her*.

As the tears spilled over, fresh panic flashed over Mitch's face. "Please don't cry. I'll stop proposing. You can ask me whenever you're ready."

Laughter bubbled up through the tears. "You don't have to ask again. I'm done running, Mitch." She tugged until he came out of the chair and leaned over her. Framing his face, she skimmed her thumbs over his cheeks and drank in his wonderful, worried face. "I love you. It's what I should've said instead of sneaking out on you. I love you, and I want to marry you."

His eyes flared even as his fingers curled gently around her wrists. "Yes? That's really a yes? It's not just the head injury talking?"

Seeing his uncertainty settled the last of her own doubts. "Not just the head injury and not the hormones."

"Thank God. Plan D involved a flash mob of 'Take A Chance On Me', and I really didn't want to go there."

Tess's mouth dropped open. "Really? I might have to change my mind just so I can see that."

"No! No takesies backsies! You said yes. You're in it now."

"Yes, I am." She drew him down, until his brow pressed lightly to hers. Her bruised head protested, but she didn't pull away. "I can't promise I'll get it all right or that I won't freak out. But I promise I love you, and I'm willing to do whatever it takes to make it work."

"We'll figure it out together."

He lowered his mouth to hers, kissing her with a gentle sweetness that undid her. They were going to be okay. Better than okay. They were going to be a family.

A throat cleared from the doorway.

Miranda stood there, a chart in her hands. "First off, sorry for intruding. But I figured you would want to know as soon as possible. I talked with Dr. Phillips and reviewed the tests myself. Everything came back clear. We'll want to follow the usual protocols tonight to keep an eye on that concussion, but you and the baby are going to be fine."

Tess sank back against the pillows. "Thank God."

"Second, congratulations, and I'm sorry."

Mitch frowned and shifted as if to block her from whatever was coming. "Sorry? For what?"

"Because the news of your pregnancy just hit the high-speed track of the gossip train. The Casserole Patrol are here volunteering today and overheard you at the nurse's station. It'll be all over town before Tess is discharged."

Mitch groaned. "Man. So much for keeping a low profile."

Tess squeezed his hand. "It's fine. We weren't going to be able to keep it a secret much longer anyway." And she was grateful they didn't have to hide anymore.

"On the plus side, they're already in heavy debate about who's knitting the baby blanket, booties, and hat."

This was life in Wishful. It was crazy and it was different, but Tess thought it would be pretty amazing. "Does that mean we've effectively distracted them from Norah and Cam?"

"I'd say yes."

"Then I'm guessing they owe us one."

Miranda grinned. "Oh, big brother, you picked a good one. She's gonna fit into this family just fine."

Tess tipped her head to Mitch's shoulder and realized Miranda was absolutely right. She did fit, and maybe that was the biggest surprise of all.

EPILOGUE

"*I*t won't be long now. The baby's head is low and you're at nine centimeters and fully effaced. I'm thinking it'll be twenty, thirty minutes before you can push." Dr. Jenkins patted Tess on the foot. "I'll be back to check on you again in a little bit."

"I can't believe we're about to meet Ulysses Barton."

"Not a chance in hell," Tess snarled, clamping down on Mitch's hand and breathing through the next contraction. "Besides, it might be a girl." In an attempt to be less rigid and plan obsessed, she'd opted not to find out.

"Well then, Nikita Xena." At her bland stare, he just grinned. "What? They're strong female role models."

Tess just shook her head and continued to breathe until the contraction passed. She couldn't quite believe the whole, wild ride was nearly over either. Despite their somewhat tumultuous beginning, she and Mitch had built that foundation. Her fiancé, as it turned out, kinda had a lock on that. He'd been her rock through the entire pregnancy, never once pressing the issue of the wedding. He'd left it entirely up to her, content having his ring on her finger.

At first, she'd waited because she'd needed time to settle into the idea. Then, they'd been overwhelmed with baby planning and finalizing renovations on the small business incubator. By the time the official ribbon cutting ceremony was through, she felt like a hippopotamus and couldn't imagine waddling down the aisle. There was no couture on earth that would've made those wedding pictures something she ever wanted to see again.

But as the next contraction hit and her husband-to-be continued chattering on with the most ridiculous names—and dear God, how had they not actually settled on *real ones* in all these months?—Tess wondered what the hell she'd been waiting for. She loved this man beyond reason.

The spasm let loose and she slumped back, grateful when he offered her some water. "You're doing great, baby."

"I want to get married," she gasped.

Mitch grinned, his dimple flashing. Oh how she hoped their baby got that dimple. "Whenever you want."

"Now."

He laughed and set the water aside. "I think you're a little busy at the moment."

"I'm not kidding."

Sobering, he shifted around to face her on the bed. "Tess, honey, you're in labor."

As far as she was concerned, that gave her a countdown clock. "Don't care. I'm a Peyton. We always get what we want. You know this."

"Baby, I appreciate that, but I'm not sure even you can hold back labor."

She fisted a hand in the front of his shirt, knowing she probably looked crazed and not caring. "Watch me." At this moment, she couldn't think of anything more important than making sure she was a proper Campbell before this baby came into the world.

Mitch blew out a breath, apparently grasping the seriousness of the order. Those hazel eyes lit with determination. "I'll see what I can do." He kissed her hard and fast and slipped out of the room.

Tess groaned her way through three more contractions while he was gone. They were getting closer together. Only three minutes apart now.

A nurse came in to check her again.

"You're at ten centimeters. It's time! I'll go get Dr. Jenkins."

Gritting her teeth, Tess dug in her heels. "I'm not having this baby yet."

Flashing her a disbelieving look, the nurse didn't reply before she left the room.

Don't argue with the crazy lady. Smart.

The door opened again and Mitch strode in, with Sandy, Trey, Cam and Norah in tow. Tess could see the rest of the family huddled in the doorway.

"Um…" The business end of things was facing away but this was a lot of people she hadn't planned on being here at this moment.

Beaming, Mitch took her hand in his. "So one of the things Aunt Sandy can do as mayor is officiate weddings."

"Nobody's ever asked me to do it before."

He'd actually found a way to pull this off. "I love you so much."

"Back atcha."

"Excuse me. Excuse me. Who are all of you?" Dr. Jenkins pushed through the mass of Campbells.

"Sorry, that's our family," Mitch explained.

"Too many cooks in this kitchen." Dr. Jenkins shot a disapproving look at all of them.

"They stay until we're married," Tess insisted.

"Married?"

"Yeah, we're having a wedding right now. My aunt is officiating."

"Well now I've seen everything." She settled on a stool at the end of the bed. "Get to it then, because we're running short on time here. This baby is coming now."

The next contraction stole Tess's breath. She felt the difference, the reality that she was just about to tip over the top for that final roller coaster drop. The pressure and intense urge to push was about to outweigh everything else. It was now or never.

Gasping, she laid her head against Mitch's shoulder. "Okay, let's do this thing."

"I don't have my official notes, so I'm gonna wing it." Sandy smiled at both of them. "We are gathered here in the sight of God and the presence of these witnesses to join together this man and this woman in holy matrimony."

"You're gonna want to do the abridged version," Dr. Jenkins warned.

"Okay then. Do you Mitch, take Tess to be your lawfully wedded wife? Will you love her, honor her, and keep her in sickness and in health and forsaking all others so long as you both shall live?"

"I will."

"Okay Tess, when this next contraction hits, I'm gonna need you to bear down and push."

"Got it."

"Do you, Tess, take Mitch to be your lawfully wedded husband? Will you love him, honor him, and keep him in sickness and in health and forsaking all others so long as you both shall live?"

"I will...ooooh holy shit!" Tess clamped down on his hands as the shock wave of pain rippled through her body.

"Breathe, baby. I'm right here with you."

"Push!"

"Not. Yet," she gritted out. "Finish it."

"Oh, oh, now the vows. Do you have any written?" Sandy asked.

"Are you kidding me?" Mitch asked.

"Okay, improvise. Repeat after me. I, Mitch, take you Tess, to be my wedded wife." She reeled off some variation of every classic movie vow ever.

Shifting around so he could look into her eyes, Mitch repeated them. "—for better, for worse, for richer, for poorer, in sickness and in health, to love and to cherish 'til death do us part." Not a single waver.

Despite the waves of pain and stress coursing through her system, a rush of pure love for this man swept over her. Tess got halfway through her own vows before the next contraction hit. She screamed her way through the end of them, and this time there was no stopping that wave.

"It's crowning! Look at that thick head of hair!"

"Oh my God, it's happening." Mitch swayed a little.

"Don't you dare pass out on me," Tess snarled.

"Wouldn't dream of it. I love you. You've got this."

"Tess, honey, you need to bear down with everything you've got," Dr. Jenkins ordered.

"We're gonna just fast forward to the end. By the authority vested in me by the state of Mississippi and the office of Mayor, I now pronounce you husband and wife."

It was official. She was a Campbell, and it was time to bring this baby into the world. Knees pulled up to her shoulders, she bore down with all her might.

"The head's out. Stop pushing, Tess, for just a second. I'm just going to clear the baby's nose and mouth." The doctor made some adjustment to the baby's position. "Okay, one more push."

She pushed, and the baby slid right out into Dr. Jenkins's waiting hands.

"Time of birth 13:48." Hands gently supporting the baby's head and butt, she raised the tiny figure into the air. "Congratulations, you two! It's a girl!"

The baby let out an offended wail, as if she disapproved of the fanfare. Tess laughed through the tears she hadn't noticed.

"Holy shit, we have a daughter," Mitch breathed.

"Here we go, Mama." Dr. Jenkins laid the baby on Tess's chest.

The baby blinked up at her with wide blue eyes. She was so

tiny, and the love welling up in Tess's heart was so huge.

"Hi. Hi there. I'm your mama." She looked up to find tears streaming down her new husband's face. "This is your Daddy."

He reached out a trembling finger to stroke the baby's cheek. "Hey, baby girl. Hey there, Vivi."

"Vivi?"

"I was thinking Vivi Anne. We're big on using family names in the south."

"Vivi Anne Campbell." Tess tested the sound of it and smiled. "That's perfect."

"I think you can kiss the bride now—ow!"

"Shut up! They're having a moment."

Tess couldn't tell who was talking and didn't care. She was too focused on Mitch as he grinned down at her.

"The peanut gallery is not wrong. I love you."

As he reached out to cup Tess's cheek, bending to press his lips to hers, she realized they'd really done it. They got married. And she couldn't imagine a more perfect beginning to the rest of forever.

∾

Choose Your Next Romance!

REMEMBER our sweet waitress Hannah Wheeler? She's up next in the Wishful lineup. Her story, *A Lot Like Christmas*, features plenty of Casserole Patrol and is certain to brighten the heart of even the grinchest of Grinches—including Army Ranger Ryan Malone.

If you'd rather pop over and read Miranda's story, then take a walk on the slightly shadowier side of Wishful with *Can't Take My Eyes Off You*, Book 3 in the Wishing for a Hero series. This one includes derring do, public serenading, and plenty of interfering Campbells.

Can't decide? Keep turning the pages for a sneak peek of both!

SNEAK PEEK A LOT LIKE CHRISTMAS

BOOK # 11 WISHFUL ROMANCE

Jaded Army medic Ryan Malone never expected his next mission would bring him back from Afghanistan to tiny Wishful, Mississippi. His great uncle's health is failing and the cantankerous old coot has pushed everyone in the family away. Ryan is their last resort to get Uncle Myron to move into assisted living before he breaks a hip--or something worse. He's looking to get in, get it done, and get back out. That definitely doesn't include taking time out for a sweet-faced waitress with a heart bigger than the Atlantic.

Interior designer Hannah Wheeler is a long way from the high-powered clients of her old Atlanta firm. Despite the fact that she's currently spending her days waiting tables, she's discovered she really enjoys the small town life she found with her sister. This Christmas season, she's finally ready to introduce Wishful to her true capabilities by using her skills to spread some holiday spirit. But with the Malone men, she's definitely got her work cut out for her.

Will Hannah's evergreen cheer thaw their frosty hearts and remind the two that the most important part of the holidays is family?

~

Chapter One

"Sugar, are you tying *utensils* on that Christmas tree?"

Undeterred by the *Girl, you crazy* tone, Hannah Wheeler finished attaching the dessert fork to a branch with a short piece of jute and shot a look over her shoulder at Omar Buckley, official master of the kitchens at Dinner Belles Diner. Taking advantage of the mid-afternoon lull, he leaned against the counter and watched her with undisguised bafflement.

"You can't judge until I'm done. Trust me." By the time she finished with the tree, the whole thing would be cute, kitchy, and scream "diner." It was just the first phase in her holiday plan to introduce Wishful to the skills she had besides carting trays and taking orders. The phase that would hopefully prove to them—and to herself—that she had the chops to pursue the rest of her revised dream.

Janelle Duncan, the other waitress on duty, was a lot more interested in checking out Omar and his former running back's body than in Hannah's efforts at decorating. Hannah wasn't overly concerned with the lack of cheerleading. In her previous life, she'd had far more difficult clients to please, and she'd always come through in the end. She'd learned that people usually didn't have any vision until someone showed it to them. And that was fine. Hannah had enough vision for all of them.

Grabbing a spoon and more jute, she turned back to the tree and jolted. A man stood on the other side of the window, peering inside. Hannah could hardly see his eyes past the scruff of a beard and the oily, matted hair. His shoulders were hunched against the unseasonably cold weather, and no wonder. The thin denim jacket—worn and stained—was hardly sufficient for the early December temperatures. Seeing the Army green duffle over his shoulder, her heart softened. She had a particular weakness for down-on-their-luck veterans. Offering a friendly smile, she waved for him to come inside.

He blinked at her, expression unchanging, still standing there with a totally unnatural stillness that said he'd been a soldier. Hannah pointed at him and mimed drinking from a cup of coffee. She hoped he took it for the invitation it was and not as some kind of pity. Amping up the smile, she waited. She'd yet to meet the man who could turn away from that smile. Certainly, it had worked to keep her dad wrapped around her little finger from the time she was knee high.

The stranger was no exception. He strode to the door and came inside, stopping just inside the threshold and scanning the room. She was pretty sure in a matter of seconds he knew where all the exits were; had noted her, Omar, and Janelle, as well as the two other patrons; and probably knew where any weapons were likely to be. Or maybe she'd just watched the Bourne movies too many times.

Hannah rose from her crouch beside the tree and held out a hand in welcome. "Please, have a seat. Warm up." Taking a few steps closer to gesture toward a corner booth she knew would have the best visibility in the place, she noted the powerful smell of unwashed body.

He must be homeless. Bless his heart. Hannah had seen it often enough when she'd lived in Atlanta, but here in Wishful, she hadn't run across it. Keeping the smile firmly in place as he sat, back to the wall, she asked, "What can I get you?"

"Just coffee," he rasped in a voice that sounded rusty with disuse.

"Coming right up." With practiced efficiency, Hannah retrieved the coffee pot and turned over the waiting ceramic mug at the table, filling it just high enough that there was room to doctor it, if he were so inclined, though she figured a guy like him would drink it black.

He grunted something that sounded like "Thanks" and wrapped his hands around the mug. The skin of his knuckles was chapped with cold.

"Can I interest you in some pie? Mama Pearl makes the best pie in six counties. The pecan in particular is to die for." Hannah leaned in conspiratorially. "But, really, the coconut cream is my favorite."

His gaze slid over to the pie rack on the counter before he shook his head.

Hannah didn't let the smile slip. "Okay then. You just let me know if you need anything."

She replaced the coffee pot and circled around the counter and into the kitchen, where Omar had resumed his post at the grill. "Be a doll and dish up one of the specials."

"Didn't hear him order the special."

"He didn't. I'm giving it to him anyway. It can come out of my tips."

He gave her an indulgent smile. "Whatever you say, Marshmallow."

Janelle shot a look through the kitchen window toward his table and kept her voice low. "You sure you want to do anything to encourage him to stay? What if he's not right in the head?"

"Don't be ridiculous," Hannah snapped, gesturing toward Omar. "That's like making the assumption that Omar is a thug because he wears a do rag and likes rap music. It's not only rude, it shows an exceptional lack of compassion." She snatched up the bowl of loaded potato soup so fast the garlic bread stick flew off the plate and onto the stainless steel counter. Blowing out a breath, Hannah carefully replaced the bread and pushed back out front, working to readjust her expression as she went. Sometimes people just killed her with their ignorance.

The stranger's brows drew together as she slid the bowl in front of him. "I didn't order this."

Hannah just smiled. "I know. But you look frozen through, so I figured you could use it. On me. And thank you for your service."

The frown was just about the only part of his expression she could see as he stared at her. Then he nodded in thanks and picked up a spoon.

Hannah left him to his meal, making a quick circuit to check on the other two customers before returning to her decorating. He'd dug into his soup with gusto by then. As she continued tying silverware to the pre-lit tree, she wondered what his story was. He definitely had that whole *Don't Pry* blinking in neon above his head. Was he passing through? Wishful wasn't exactly on the way to anywhere.

As she made a fresh pass to top off his coffee, the stranger looked up. "Is there a garage around here?"

Hannah had to think about that a moment. She didn't drive, so she wasn't as familiar with those details as she otherwise would be. "We have two that I know of." She tried to think which one would be more likely hiring. "Lou Perkins is over on Grantham Street, about three blocks that way." Hannah pointed toward the north end of the town green. "His nephew just got his second DUI and was shipped off to rehab a couple weeks ago, so he's a little short-handed. And then there's Benny Wills's place on the west side of town." She offered up some quick directions there as well. "There's a gorgeous restored Chevelle sitting out front. You can't miss it."

He watched her for another long moment with that inscrutable gaze before finally saying, "Thanks."

The bowl of soup had all but been licked clean. Hannah gestured to it. "Can I get that out of your way?"

The stranger nodded, so she scooped up the dishes with her free hand.

"Sure I can't talk you into some pie?"

"Not right now. Thanks."

She just nodded. "Endless refills on coffee. You stay as long as you like."

~

THOUGH he really needed to get moving, Sergeant Ryan Malone lingered over his coffee and surreptitiously watched the waitress as she continued to decorate the diner's Christmas tree, both because he was wondering how the hell it would turn out all loaded with forks and spoons and because he kept expecting to catch a glimpse of elf ears through that fall of dark hair. She'd make a good elf with that fine-boned face and fair skin. She hummed while she worked, the edge of a smile just waiting to bow up those full lips. How could anybody over the age of ten be that unrelentingly cheerful and innocent? She made him feel ancient at twenty-seven, though she was probably close to his age.

Ryan strained to hear the tune and finally recognized "It's Beginning To Look A Lot Like Christmas." Certainly the rest of what he'd seen of Wishful fit the bill. As he'd come into the downtown area, he'd noted the holiday decorations mounted on all the light poles and the twinkle lights wrapped around the denuded trees lining Main Street. People bustled along the sidewalk, toting shopping bags and pretty, wrapped packages. It was about as far as he could get from the war zone he'd been walking in mere days ago, and the switch had him feeling more off balance than the jet lag.

Across the room, Elf Girl plugged in the lights and the tree lit up.

Well, I'll be damned.

The glow of the white twinkle lights bounced off the silverware and gave the tree a warm, inviting glow. Who would've thought utensils would make good ornaments for a Christmas tree?

Elf Girl stepped back, crossing her arms and smiling in satisfaction. That smile did something to a man. Certainly it had done something to him. He'd had no intention of stopping in the diner. None at all. Then she'd flashed those dimples at him, and he'd been pulled inside as if she were a kerosene heater that could thaw his frozen hands and feet.

She'd thought he was homeless. He sure as hell looked it after traveling for three days straight to get from Bumfuck, Afghanistan to here. God knew when he'd last shaved. Exhaustion had carved lines around his eyes. He'd been awake way too damned long even before he boarded the MAC flight back to Fort Polk, where he'd picked up the rust bucket of a truck he'd borrowed from a friend still overseas. Smitty had sworn the thing was ugly but sound and would get him the six hours to Wishful. Ryan had believed him—until the ancient Chevy began to sputter and wheeze when he was nearly to his destination. The truck had crapped out eight miles from town.

Ryan had left in such a hurry, he had little with him other than his duffle. Not even a coat to face the frigid December weather. And since when was it this freaking cold in Mississippi in December? He'd found an ancient and smelly jacket shoved behind the seat. It had all kinds of questionable stains, but it was another layer against the chill, so he'd put it on and started walking to town. No doubt that hadn't helped with the impression of homelessness either.

Too many people would've looked through him, pretending he wasn't there, or gotten nervy, like the other waitress that'd been hiding in the kitchen since he walked in. But not the elf. Her instinct had been to bring bring him in out of the cold, warm him up, and feed him. She'd looked him straight in the eye and hadn't even balked at the stench of the jacket. Wasn't that interesting?

Nice to know there were people like her out there in the world, even if he himself wasn't in need of her kindness.

Well, he was thawed out now, and he was losing daylight. If he was gonna get by one of the garages to see about getting a tow, he needed to get moving. Waiting until Elf Girl slipped through the door to the kitchen, Ryan pulled out a wad of cash and left a ridiculous tip—more than enough to cover the soup and coffee—then headed out into the cold.

As it had sounded closer, he took a chance on Lou Perkins's place, trudging north along the town green until he located Grantham Street. The garage wasn't hard to find, and the tow truck he desperately needed was parked right out front. The bay doors were closed, but the single door to the office part of the building was unlocked, so Ryan ducked inside. The office was empty. Some kind of hard rock Christmas music blared from the garage. Following the music, he tugged open another door and stepped into the work space. A pair of legs was visible beneath an older model Ford Escort. The work boots tapped in time with the music as their owner sang along with more enthusiasm than skill.

"Hello?" Ryan called.

The feet stopped twitching and the creeper shot out from beneath the car. A skinny, balding man with a graying goatee peered up at him. "What can I do ya for?"

"Was hoping you could hook me up with a tow and some repairs. My truck broke down about eight miles from here."

The older man's dark eyes skimmed him from head to toe as he sat up. "You walk all the way here?"

"Yes, sir."

"Reckon you could use some coffee. Pot's on in the office. I gotta finish up here in the next little bit, 'fore Betsy Maynard swings by to pick this puppy up." He tapped the bumper of the Escort. "Then we'll see what there is to see."

Ryan thought about calling Percy. But that'd blow the element of surprise, and given the family's reports of his behavior lately,

Ryan wasn't quite ready to give up that advantage. Resigned to waiting, he just nodded. It'd take less time to do this than to hunt up the other garage. And he was really damned tired. Retreating back to the office, he set down his bag and took one of the thinly padded chairs.

"Hey fella."

Ryan tripped from sleep to wakefulness in an instant, his hand reaching for the combat knife he wasn't actually wearing at the moment.

The mechanic stood a good three paces away, hands lifted in the universal sign for no threat. "Army?"

"Yes, sir." Ryan forced his muscles to relax. Damn, he must've been more exhausted than he thought if he hadn't heard the other man enter the room.

"Navy," the mechanic said. "Thirty years ago, now. You have the look aboutcha. Ready to go pick up that truck?"

The two of them loaded into the tow truck and Ryan directed the mechanic—who was, in fact, Lou himself—to where he'd left the Chevy on the little two-lane highway. Quick and efficient, Lou had the truck hooked up and towed back to the garage in less than an hour. Then he went the extra mile and dropped Ryan off at Percy's on his way home. Apparently Elf Girl wasn't the only person in town willing to go out of their way to help a stranger.

Shouldering his bag, Ryan strode up the walk toward the house. The porch was dark, but a light shone from somewhere in the back. He pressed the bell, listening to the tones of it ring and fade before a faint voice hollered, "I'm coming. I'm coming!"

Ryan waited, wondering exactly what to say since he hadn't called ahead. Before he could decide, a loud crash sounded from inside.

"Percy?" Ryan shouted. He banged on the door, tested the knob. Locked. He checked the immediate vicinity for a key. Finding none and given the reports his mom had passed along about the state of Percy's health, he dropped his bag, took a step back, and kicked in the front door.

The lock gave way with a snap, the door flying back to hit the interior wall. Ryan charged through with all the speed and efficiency of his Delta Force training, clearing rooms until he found the old man on his knees, one hand braced on the arm of a sofa as he struggled to rise. A lamp lay on the floor, the cattywampus shade casting crazy shadows on the wall.

A quick flash of fear crossed the old man's face before he firmed his expression. "Who the hell are you and what are you doing in my house?"

Ryan picked up the lamp and righted it before offering a hand. "Good to see you too, Uncle Percy."

Get yours today!

SNEAK PEEK CAN'T TAKE MY EYES OFF YOU

BOOK #3 WISHING FOR A HERO

Exhausted by the futility of her efforts against the city's endemic problems and the revolving door of violence in her Chicago emergency room, Dr. Miranda Campbell came home to Wishful, where she knew she could make a real difference in people's lives. Between her clinic, a rotation in the hospital's ER, volunteer work at the new women's shelter, and time spent with family and friends, her life is full. But it's not too full to notice a sexy lawman when she sees one.

Former US Marshal Ethan Greer is still settling into the job as Wishful's new Chief of Police, but he's starting to realize it may be years before he'll ever be considered one of the locals. Fair enough. He's the first to admit that making the shift to small town policing is a big adjustment. After losing his marriage and almost his life in line of duty, the slow pace of Wishful is a change he's happy to make.

While Miranda's and Ethan interest in each other is mutual, he's not sure about taking on a serious relationship. That's just fine with her. But when Miranda is targeted in an escalating chain of threatening events, Ethan's Marshal instincts go on overdrive. Miranda's rose-colored view of Wishful is putting her in danger. She's become more than a casual fling or a job responsibility. With Ethan's training screaming at him to put her in protective custody, can he find out who's behind the threats before he pushes Miranda away?

~

CHAPTER ONE

"*H*ey, hey married lady." Miranda Campbell grinned as her best friend slid into the opposite side of the booth.

"Someday that will probably get old, but it is not this day," Norah declared. "Sorry I'm late. Meeting ran over."

Miranda noted her faintly mussed hair and rosy cheeks and smirked. "And did your *meeting* come to a satisfactory conclusion? Judging from your glow, I'm gonna guess it did."

Norah cast a frantic look around, her just-had-a-quickie-with-my-new-hubby glow being replaced by a ferocious blush. "Keep your voice down!" she hissed.

"Hey, at least one of us is being kept satisfied. I just try not to think too hard about the fact that it's my cousin putting that look on your face. Did you and Cam at least remember to lock the door this time?"

"That was *one* time."

Miranda just arched a brow.

"Okay, maybe two." Norah dropped her voice. "He has a thing about desks."

Lifting a hand Miranda shook her head. "Stop right there. I don't need to know this." At Norah's chagrined expression, she added, "But it's awesome to still see you blissfully happy. You're practically radioactive with contentment."

Norah unwound her scarf and shed the red wool coat, running her hands through her dark brown hair to neaten it. "I'm going to credit the happy for making me susceptible to crazy proposals."

"Is that a euphemism for something?"

Norah laughed. "No. But somehow I find myself chairing the committee organizing the Valentine's Dance this year. Because I have so much spare time, right?"

And then it all came suddenly clear. Bracing both hands on the table, Miranda stared her down. "You invited me to lunch to talk me onto that committee didn't you?"

"It'll be fun!"

Unamused, Miranda just continued to stare.

"What's that face, Dr. Campbell?" Mama Pearl, the much-beloved heart and soul of Dinner Belles Diner, slid their customary sweet teas onto the table.

Miranda gestured across the table. "Norah here has been whacked upside the head with the love stick and thinks she's gonna talk me onto the Valentine's Dance committee."

"If I had to judge by the smile she was wearin' when she walked in here, I'd say there was definitely a love stick involved."

Norah's mouth fell open. "Mama Pearl, hush your mouth!"

Miranda snickered and a grin creased the older woman's dark face.

"Usual?"

"Yes, ma'am," they chorused.

As soon as she shuffled off, Norah resumed her campaign. "Anyway, it'll be the social event of the season."

That wasn't saying much. With a population just edging toward six thousand people, Wishful wasn't exactly a hopping, happening place. Social gatherings down here tended more toward church potlucks, football parties, and chilling out at The Mudcat Tavern. Miranda was totally okay with that. Transforming the community center into something out of a John Hughes movie prom set for a town-wide dance was not her idea of a good time. Or maybe that was just a little sour grapes because she wouldn't have anyone to go with.

"I already made my contribution to the Wishful social calendar for the year with my annual New Year's Eve bash. Literally last week."

"And that bash was awesome," Norah conceded. "But come on. It'll be like the old days back in college, when we were planning sorority mixers."

"I do not have the enticement of half a dozen cute Sigma Chis doing set up for this."

"So if I can load the setup crew with hot single men for you to ogle, you'll do it?"

Miranda knew she'd make it happen. She also knew Norah would just keep pushing until she got what she wanted. "It is my busiest season at the clinic. Flu is horrific this year, and I'm trying to control an outbreak of strep. I cannot commit to committee meetings. But I'm available for brainstorming, and I promise to clear the decks as much as I can for actual setup. Final offer."

"Deal."

"Hey, y'all."

Miranda looked up to find her administrative assistant hovering at the edge of the table. She braced herself. "Please tell me Shelby didn't send you to fetch me for an emergency at the clinic." She desperately needed this hour to check out with her best gal pal and breathe something that wasn't disinfectant fumes and illness.

Delaney laughed. "Nope. Here to pick up takeout for me and Keisha. Did I hear y'all talking about the Valentine's Dance?"

"Oh girl, you have made a grave error," Miranda told her. "Run, run now, before you get sucked in."

Norah beamed a bright smile Delaney's way. "You sure did. Are you interested in joining the committee?"

"Um, I don't know. What would it entail?"

Miranda just shook her head as Norah cheerfully and skillfully herded Delaney right where she wanted her. Which was what Norah Burke Crawford did. Nobody ever saw it coming. At her high-powered marketing firm in Chicago, that talent had earned her the moniker The Closer. It was a skill Miranda both abhorred and admired. Since Norah used it to the benefit of the town these days, Miranda was hardly in a position to complain. At least until Norah turned those skills on her. Thankfully, long familiarity gave her some measure of immunity.

Amused, she watched Norah go in for the kill.

"It's a great way to give back to the community."

Delaney grinned. "Sounds great. Sign me up."

"Wonderful! We'll see you on Tuesday for our first meeting."

"Okay then. Bye, Miranda."

"See you back at the clinic."

She and Norah both watched as the younger woman headed for the counter to pick up her order.

"Never even saw what hit her."

"How's she working out for you?" Norah asked. "You've had her—what?—three months now?"

"Really well. We had a few hiccups that first week, but she's a quick learner and a hard worker. Shelby's ecstatic to have help running the office. Especially somebody to take over the onerous management of the computer system. You know how Shelby hates that thing."

"—just can't believe she has the nerve to walk around with her head held high after what she did."

Miranda didn't even have to scan the busy diner for the speaker. Clarice Hopper Morris was a bitch on wheels and had been since elementary school. If there was something cruel to be said about someone, she or her sister had no compunction in saying it. At the counter, Delaney's shoulders tensed and rounded, as if she could make herself a smaller target. Miranda's temper bubbled and snapped on the girl's behalf as Clarice and her companion just kept right on talking.

"I'm surprised they didn't run her out of town on a rail after it happened."

"Didn't she get arrested or somethin'?"

"Well, you know she did. It was all over the paper. Don't know what she's doing back in Wishful."

Miranda's fists clenched as Delaney paid for her lunch, took the takeout bag, and all but ran out of the diner.

Mama Pearl shook her head as she slid two plates onto the table and looked after Delaney. She shot a fulminating look at the gossipers and announced in a voice they couldn't fail to hear, "Anybody can change."

Clarice didn't pay any attention to Mama Pearl. "I can't imagine what she's doing for work. I mean, who on earth would hire her after everything she did?"

Temper bubbling, Miranda shoved out of the booth and marched across the diner. "That would be me, and I'll thank you to stop spreading malicious gossip about my employee."

Clarice and her companion, Karen Alberson, looked up in shock.

"Why Miranda Campbell. I didn't realize your charity work ran to your employees, too. How...magnanimous of you."

Steam was most certainly coming out of her ears. Miranda itched to plow her bunched fist into Clarice's face. "I suppose you would think it magnanimous to recognize that sometimes people make mistakes and deserve a second chance. The fact of the matter is, she's a smart girl and a hard worker, and she deserves better than to be maligned by the likes of you."

"It's a free country. There's no law against talking."

"Sadly, no, there's no law against being hateful. If there were, you and your sister would both have rap sheets taller than either of you." Disgusted, Miranda shook her head. "Are your lives so bad, you feel the need to talk down about everybody around? Tearing down good people and perpetuating rumors and half-truths about the mistakes they may have made to make yourselves feel better?"

"I hardly think our topics of conversation are any of your business."

"I think you know you're making it everyone's business by talking loud enough for the whole diner to hear you, just to get attention. Grow up, Clarice. And maybe you could find a scrap of humanity while you're at it." Miranda swung around to go back to the booth for the lunch she no longer wanted and plowed straight into a brick wall.

The wall gripped her elbows and drawled, "Steady there."

Startled, she looked up...and up, into the clearest gray eyes she'd ever seen.

CHIEF OF POLICE Ethan Greer had dealt with a lot of angry people in his lifetime. It wasn't generally an attractive state, often involving red faces and flying spittle—or fists. But Miranda Campbell, in full temper, facing off with a couple of women he'd already learned were bitchy gossips even in his short three months on the job, was one of the most unaccountably sexy things he'd ever beheld. Ethan had no idea who she was defending, but those changeable hazel eyes still flashed with a righteous indignation as she looked up at him. Stunning.

As they stood there, the indignation faded and something else pulsed between them. It had been so damned long, Ethan barely recognized it for what it was. Mutual attraction. And wasn't that interesting?

"Excuse me, Chief."

"Doc."

Her eyes widened slightly at that. Yeah, he knew who she was, even if they hadn't actually spoken before. At 5'10", with a fall of thick, honey blonde hair a man could lose his hands in, she was a hard woman not to notice.

Ethan released her, edging back so she could get by him. He shifted his attention to the gossips, leveling them with the flat cop stare that tended to make hardened criminals break. The side-kick's cheeks reddened, and she looked down at the table. The ash blonde with the pinched face, who'd been doing most of the talk-ing, just lifted a brow. Supercilious bitch. He knew the type. For the sake of whoever she'd been maligning, he wished he did have something he could arrest her for. She needed to be knocked down a few pegs.

"Hey Chief. Are you meeting somebody or sitting at the counter today?"

He found a smile for the fresh-faced waitress, who'd arrived in Wishful not long after he had. "Mornin', Hannah. I'm meetin' Clay."

"There's a booth right over here." She led him to the opposite side of the diner from Miranda. "I'll just get your tea."

As he sat, studying the menu, conversation started up again. That whole confrontation was gonna be all over town by dinner. Probably faster. He'd learned that viral social media had nothing on the gossip network in Wishful. Especially when it started here, at Mama Pearl's place. If you wanted to know anything, Dinner Belles was the first place you started.

Clay wandered in and worked his way toward the table, pausing in time-honored, small-town tradition to greet everyone he knew. Given Wishful was his hometown, that was most of them. The delay was fine with Ethan. It gave him a chance to surreptitiously watch the good doctor as she conversed with City Planner Norah Crawford.

Clay slid into the other side of the booth. "See somethin' you like?"

Or maybe not so surreptitiously. "Hello to you, too."

Hannah came back with his tea. "Hey Clay."

"Miss Hannah Wheeler. And how are you this fine day?"

Ethan wondered if there was a woman between twelve and eighty in this town that his best friend didn't know by name.

"Doing fine. Caught your show last weekend. Nice to know the rumors are true. You're good."

He grinned. "Glad you enjoyed it. You know, I used to be a part of a duo."

Her brown eyes brightened with interest. "Yeah? What happened?"

Clay turned a bland stare on Ethan. "My partner went off and joined law enforcement."

"And you became a high school math teacher," Ethan shot back.

Hannah stared. "You, Chief? Really?"

Shifting in the booth, Ethan shrugged. "It was a long time ago."

"Well, that is a thing I'd like to see." She lifted her order pad. "What can I get you?"

"What can you do about a bacon cheeseburger?" Clay shot her the twenty-four carat smile that girls had been fawning over since he was a cocky nineteen-year-old. It hadn't lost its potency.

Hannah blushed and batted her eyes in his direction. "I'll get Omar right on that. You want onion straws on it like your usual?"

"That'd be great. And a Coke."

She made a note on her order pad. "How 'bout you, Chief?"

Mentally adding an extra mile to tomorrow's morning run, Ethan stuck the menu back between the napkin dispenser and the ketchup. "I'll have the same."

"You got it."

As soon as she'd wandered away, Clay started in. "So when am I gonna get you back up on stage?"

Here we go again.

"I've been trying to get settled into this new job, establishing myself in the community. I need people to see me as Chief of Police before they see me on stage."

"It's been three months, man. You're in it, you're settled, and I promise you everybody knows exactly who you are."

"Yeah, the new guy." The new guy who was still in a probationary period for another nine months. Despite the fact that his transition had gone pretty smoothly, Ethan was sure the jury was still out for a lot of people. He was an outsider here.

From the corner of his eye, Ethan noted the gossips packing up and heading out. His eyes slid to Miranda. She scowled after the pair, muttering something under her breath and stabbing at her lunch with more savagery than necessary.

"Getting your ass back on stage and showing folks you can be approachable would go a long way toward being something other than the new guy."

Ethan dragged his attention back to Clay. "Yeah, I remember how people treated me when we performed back in college. That's not the kind of approachable I want to be."

Clay laid a hand over his heart. "Those were the days. But unlike you, I've been performing all the years in between, and it's been at least a few months since anybody threw their underwear on the stage." At Ethan's cop stare, he sobered. "Seriously though, Wishful isn't a college town, so people aren't gonna behave like they did in Austin. The Mudcat is the kind of small, intimate venue you used to love to play."

Back when it had been entirely about the music. Yeah, Ethan couldn't deny that had some appeal. He still played for himself and had occasionally stepped out for open mic nights in Dallas, but it had been years since he and Clay had performed together. He'd be lying if he didn't admit he missed it. Hadn't he taken this job so he'd have the chance for more of a life outside work? Part of that life ought to include taking back up hobbies that didn't involve honing his skills with a gun or attending training seminars.

"All right. I'll think about it. We can at least set up some rehearsals."

Clay smirked. "Think you remember how?"

"Smartass. I may not have been on stage in ages, but I can still keep up with you."

"Great! How about you prove it Saturday?"

"Can't. I'm running a bowhunter's safety course Saturday. Maybe Sunday afternoon?"

As Hannah slid their burgers onto the table, Clay nodded, satisfied. "I can work with that."

Across the diner, Miranda and Norah rose, shrugging into coats.

"Getting back into music isn't the only thing you've been avoiding."

"What are you talking about?"

"Dating, my friend. You haven't done any of it since the divorce."

Yeah, he'd been busy trying not to die, then changing his entire life. Women hadn't exactly factored into the equation. And Ethan had been fine with that. Nobody had sparked his interest anyway.

Miranda's laugh rang out, rich and unabashed. The sound rolled over him like warm molasses.

Until now.

"She's single."

Ethan jerked his attention back to Clay. "Who?"

"Miranda. I assume you weren't eyeing the new Mrs. Crawford."

"I'm not eying anybody." But he couldn't stop himself from glancing back as the two women got to the door.

Clay continued as if he hadn't even spoken. "She's a lot of fun. Helluva dancer."

Something in the casual tone had Ethan's hackles rising. Still, he kept his expression bland and reached for the ketchup. "And you'd know that why?"

"We dated a while."

The bottle jerked in his hand, making his fries look like the victim of a particularly gruesome homicide. Stupid. He'd exchanged all of two sentences with the woman, and both of those were today. He certainly had no claim on Miranda Campbell, and he sure as shit had no right to be aggravated that she'd gone out with his best friend. "I expect you've dated damn near every single woman who's breathing in Wishful at one point or other."

"My streak isn't near as wide as you seem to think."

Ethan just lifted a brow at him.

"Not since I came home, anyway," Clay amended, grinning. "Anyway, it wasn't recent. We had some fun together, but we just didn't click."

Ethan didn't want to think about what kind of fun that might've been. "Doesn't matter one way or the other."

"So you think being Chief of Police means you don't get a love life either? Man, why did you move here again?"

"You know why."

"Yeah, and I remember something in there about having a life while you still had one. You're falling down on that, brother."

Ethan scowled at his friend. "I'm easing in at my own pace."

"Yeah, the Geriatric 500." Clay leaned closer, lowering his voice. "Look, I know Becca did a number on you. But it's time to get back out there."

The flash of honey gold hair had Ethan looking up.

As if summoned by Clay's words, Miranda stood there, those hazel eyes snapping, her long, surgeon's fingers balled to fists. "Chief Greer, I'm really sorry to interrupt your lunch, but I need to report a crime."

As Wishful's not-quite-brand-new police chief turned those clear gray eyes to hers, Miranda couldn't help but hear Clay's words repeated in her head.

It's time to get back out there.

For the barest instant, she forgot what she'd come here to talk to him about because her long neglected lady parts were busy standing up and waving. *I volunteer as tribute!*

"What happened?"

Those three little syllables pulled Miranda out of her nanosecond's fantasy about what those big, warm hands that had steadied her earlier would feel like somewhere more interesting than her elbows. She didn't have time for tributes or fantasies.

"My car's been vandalized."

He didn't look annoyed, didn't even look at his food. He just slid from the booth. "Show me."

The position put him inside her personal bubble again, and Miranda took an instinctive step back, glancing at Clay. "Sorry to borrow him."

Clay waved that off. "Nature of the job."

Ethan followed her out of the diner and halfway down the block to where she'd parked. He didn't make casual small talk. Miranda had no idea what to say, so she said nothing at all, just pointed him to her driver's side door where *Nosy Bitch* had been scratched into the paint. He still didn't speak, just slowly circled the vehicle snapping pictures and, presumably, looking for more damage.

Eventually, he brought that laser focus back to her. "Do you have any idea who might do this?"

Why did his attention make her want to shiver?

"I know exactly who did it. You walked in on the tail end of our argument earlier. Clarice Morris."

"The blonde in the diner?"

"That'd be her."

"What was the argument about?"

The temper that had dropped to a simmer cranked back up to boil. "She was maligning one of my employees. I called her out on it."

"Is this your first run-in with Ms. Morris?"

Miranda snorted. "Hardly."

Ethan's eyes sharpened at that. "You have history?"

"Going all the way back to first grade."

A flicker of surprise cracked the serious cop mask. "First grade?"

"Not an exaggeration, actually. It's a small town. Most of us go back a long way. In this case, Clarice and her sister, Amber, have a history of tearing people down. I abhor bullies, so I have, over the years, intervened to defend people. And before you ask, no, it's never led to any kind of physical blows or retaliation in this particular fashion."

"So why do you think it was her this time?"

Miranda frowned at him. "Because I literally just dressed her down in public. She left first, and I come out to find this. Two and two equals four."

He glanced back at the door. "She only had a couple minutes' lead on you. A message like this would take a little while to carve in. I'm not sure she had enough time to do it. Is there anybody else who might have a grudge against you?"

"Contrary to the evidence of the moment, I don't make it a habit to fight with people. I don't have enemies."

That focus came back to her, feeling almost like a physical touch. When Ethan Greer looked at her, he really looked *at her*. No glancing at her shoulder or the bridge of her nose. He made full, unabashed eye contact. It was both disconcerting and strangely intimate.

"Everybody has enemies, even if they don't know it."

"That's a pretty cynical point of view."

"What you call cynicism, I consider realism. Realistically, unless somebody happened to be driving by, or walking on the green and glanced over at the right moment, nobody actually saw this happen. There are no businesses with security cameras along this stretch. There's not really any way to prove who did this. You can believe down deep in your gut that this woman was behind it, but without any corroborating evidence, I can't charge her with anything."

"You're not even going to talk to her?"

"Oh, I'll talk to her. But unless she spontaneously confesses, I don't really have anything else to go on."

"So basically I dragged you away and let your lunch go cold for nothing." Scooping a hand through her hair, Miranda felt stupid. Of course there was nothing he could do about this. It was minor vandalism. He probably had more important things to be worrying about.

"Not nothing. I'll write up a report to document it. If you plan to file a claim on your insurance, you'll need that."

She blew out a breath and looked at her Jeep. Having the door repainted wouldn't eat up her deductible for the year, and reporting it would probably just make her rates go up. With the burden of her mortgage, student loans from med school, and the business loan on her practice, that was the last thing she needed.

It's an inconvenience. An irritant. Clarice just wanted to get to you, and you're giving her exactly what she wants.

With effort, Miranda tamped her temper down. She had patients to get back to, and she needed to be calm when she saw them. "Thank you."

"I'll need your number."

She blinked at him. Had he just asked her out?

"To let you know when the report is finished. The forms are all in my patrol car."

"Right." *Idiot. He's just doing his job.*

He punched the number into his phone. "It should be ready for pick up in a day or two, after I've had a chance to talk to Ms. Morris."

Not, *I'll call you.*

"I appreciate it, Chief Greer. And I apologize again for dragging you away from your lunch."

He angled his head and started to lift his hand before stopping himself, as if he was accustomed to having a hat to tip at a lady. "No problem. You have a good day now, Doc."

Miranda climbed into the driver's seat and watched him go.

Maybe she'd completely misread that frisson of attraction when they'd bumped into each other in the diner earlier. She'd been out of the dating game entirely since she came home to Wishful, and her last relationship had left her singed enough to be okay with that state of affairs. But Ethan Greer made her wonder. Worse, he made her want things she hadn't wanted in a very long time.

Doesn't matter. He's not interested, and you don't have time for a guy anyway.

But as she drove past the diner on her way back to the clinic, she couldn't stop herself from taking one more glance at the way those broad shoulders filled out his uniform shirt.

Get yours today!

OTHER BOOKS BY KAIT NOLAN

A complete and up-to-date list of all my books can be found at https://kaitnolan.com.

~

THE MISFIT INN SERIES
SMALL TOWN FAMILY ROMANCE

- *When You Got A Good Thing* (Kennedy and Xander)
- *Til There Was You* (Misty and Denver)
- *Those Sweet Words* (Pru and Flynn)
- *Stay A Little Longer* (Athena and Logan)
- *Bring It On Home* (Maggie and Porter)

RESCUE MY HEART SERIES
SMALL TOWN MILITARY ROMANCE

- *Baby It's Cold Outside* (Ivy and Harrison)
- *What I Like About You* (Laurel and Sebastian)
- *Bad Case of Loving You* (Paisley and Ty prequel)

- *Made For Loving You* (Paisley and Ty)

MEN OF THE MISFIT INN
SMALL TOWN SOUTHERN ROMANCE

- *Let It Be Me* (Emerson and Caleb)
- *Our Kind of Love* (Abbey and Kyle)

WISHFUL SERIES
SMALL TOWN SOUTHERN ROMANCE

- *Once Upon A Coffee* (Avery and Dillon)
- *To Get Me To You* (Cam and Norah)
- *Know Me Well* (Liam and Riley)
- *Be Careful, It's My Heart* (Brody and Tyler)
- *Just For This Moment* (Myles and Piper)
- *Wish I Might* (Reed and Cecily)
- *Turn My World Around* (Tucker and Corinne)
- *Dance Me A Dream* (Jace and Tara)
- *See You Again* (Trey and Sandy)
- *The Christmas Fountain* (Chad and Mary Alice)
- *You Were Meant For Me* (Mitch and Tess)
- *A Lot Like Christmas* (Ryan and Hannah)
- *Dancing Away With My Heart* (Zach and Lexi)

WISHING FOR A HERO SERIES (A WISHFUL SPINOFF SERIES)
SMALL TOWN ROMANTIC SUSPENSE

- *Make You Feel My Love* (Judd and Autumn)
- *Watch Over Me* (Nash and Rowan)
- *Can't Take My Eyes Off You* (Ethan and Miranda)
- *Burn For You* (Sean and Delaney)

MEET CUTE ROMANCE

SMALL TOWN SHORT ROMANCE

- *Once Upon A Snow Day*
- *Once Upon A New Year's Eve*
- *Once Upon An Heirloom*
- *Once Upon A Coffee*
- *Once Upon A Campfire*
- *Once Upon A Rescue*

SUMMER CAMP
CONTEMPORARY ROMANCE

- *Once Upon A Campfire*
- *Second Chance Summer*

ABOUT KAIT

Kait is a Mississippi native, who often swears like a sailor, calls everyone sugar, honey, or darlin', and can wield a bless your heart like a saber or a Snuggie, depending on requirements.

You can find more information on this RITA ® Award-winning author and her books on her website http://kaitnolan.com. While you're there, sign up for her newsletter so you don't miss out on news about new releases!

Printed in the USA
CPSIA information can be obtained
at www.ICGtesting.com
LVHW010500260424
778447LV00002B/466

9 781648 351181